THE ACCIDENTAL SENATOR

Push and Pole Series, Book 2

LAURA HEFFERNAN

Books by Laura Heffernan

The Reality Star Series

America's Next Reality Star

Sweet Reality

Reality Wedding

The Oceanic Dreams Series

Time of My Life

The Gamer Girls Series

She's Got Game

Against the Rules

Make Your Move

Push and Pole Series

Poll Dancer

The Accidental Senator

Finding Tranquility

Anna's Guide to Getting Even

To Molly,

*If I could pick anyone I know
to randomly become Senator,
it absolutely would be you.*

Not Matt.

Chapter One

Fifteen votes. Fifteen forking votes (Sorry, I'm trying to curb the swearing now that I'm a State Senator). I wasn't even running. No one's ever won with the write-in vote, have they? *Hey Siri, set reminder: Google "write-in wins."*

Never thought I'd be a trendsetter. Neither did anyone else, which is why I was voted "Least Likely to be a Trendsetter" in high school. Got way more than fifteen votes, too.

All this ran through my head as I hurried up the steps to the front door of the New York State House and through the metal detectors. Once I reclaimed my messenger bag from the conveyor belt, I looked around, desperately trying to figure out where to go for my first day. There's no big orientation following a special election like when a whole new legislature starts in January. I arrived to find quiet halls and hushed voices and an email telling me to look for my mentor. Hopefully I'd figure things out.

Like where the hashtag to find my office. Ever since I arrived at the massive building housing the state legislative offices, I'd been wandering up and down, listening to my heels clack along the floor, echoing down the halls. Although it was fairly early, I hadn't seen another soul, making me either embarrassingly late on my first day or that dork who always showed up too early.

For the third time, I consulted my phone. Jason Park, he was the person assigned to show me around. Now only if I could find—oof!

Something slammed into me. My phone hit the floor and skittered across the tile. Looking up, I found myself staring into a gorgeous pair of brown eyes framed with thick, lush black lashes. The owner of the eyes was taller than me, but not too tall, with short, spiky black hair and perfect lips. He looked muscular but not too buff. Strong and solid. Quite delicious.

"I'm so sorry," he said. "Are you Lana Chen?"

"What gave me away?"

"The name on your pass." He pointed.

Oh, right. I'd hung my ID card around my neck for lack of any better place to put it. On my first day, chances were I'd be showing the thing about four dozen times.

I grinned at him. "It labels me a newbie?"

"Nah, just makes you easy to spot." He held out one hand. "I'm Jason. Senator Park."

Hmmph. Ogling my guide wasn't the best way to start a new job. I told myself to tone it down and be professional. "Ah, yes! You must be the Asian Welcome Wagon."

His lips twitched. "Of course. And you're the stripper?"

Nope. I was not a stripper, not that there was anything wrong with that. Which my mentor probably knew. He also knew the details of the special election that brought me here. Everyone knew that the surprise candidate, my best friend Mel, taught pole fitness before her campaign started. It was, in fact, somehow the number one issue of importance to voters. It didn't surprise me that both the stigma and the inaccurate assumptions transferred to me as her best friend and a campaign advisor, especially after I won the job in her place.

I refused to lend them any credence.

"Touché," I said. "It's nice to meet you."

Jason turned around and led me down the hall to my office, pointing out various points of interest along the way. "I'm the liaison for all new Senators. It's my job to show you the ropes."

"Good to know. I left my pasties at home." I'd worn them when Mel needed me to help with a presentation, over other clothes, but whatevs.

He chuckled. "It's good that you have a sense of humor. That'll serve you well around here."

"I figure I could either make jokes or spend the day lecturing people about misogyny in the world and the dangers of slut-shaming," I said. "I don't like to lecture before I've finished my coffee. Catch me later."

Redness tinged his cheeks. Good. If I accomplished nothing else before the end of my term, I would get people to stop making women feel bad for using any assets they had to find work, including their bodies. Whether it was because they had no other choice or because they enjoyed it. Putting aside the obvious fact that men also worked as strippers and sex workers, no one would do it if there weren't people willing to pay them.

"Here we are!" Jason turned the corner and opened a door on the right side of the hallway. It stuck. He pushed again, and the door opened a couple of inches. "Sorry. We may need to call Maintenance. Something's wrong."

"Let me try." I waved him back and examined the door. I might be short, but I was strong. Resting my shoulder against the wood, I shoved with all my might.

Perhaps I overshot a little. The door flew open. Something on the other side crashed. I stumbled into the room. It took a few steps before I caught my balance, thanks largely to a mountain of cardboard blocking the path and slamming into my stomach. Oof.

"What the fork?"

Giant boxes packed the room reserved for my staff from one end to the next, in places stacked three or four high. I couldn't even see the door to my own office, which theoretically was somewhere on the right-hand wall. Words stamped on the outside of each box identified the contents as belonging to a popular line of skincare products. That couldn't be right. But then I remembered. I wound up here in the first place because my predecessor had a "revelation" of some sort. He left his wife, invested heavily in a multi-level marketing scheme, decided to sell products from an RV with his new girlfriend, and resigned.

Jason stepped into the space behind me, glancing around. "Uh…it appears Senator Baker may have left a few things behind."

Awesome. There wasn't even a way to get to the inner office, where I'd be working. My assistant's desk was completely buried. This wasn't going to work. All this junk needed to go, ASAP. Unfortunately, I didn't know where to send it. It didn't belong to me, so I couldn't just throw it away.

I didn't have a way to contact the former Senator, but I did have the number for his son Curtis. We'd gotten to know each other over the past couple of months, although it might be a stretch to call us friends. We were reasonably friendly when we found ourselves on the same side.

Texting wouldn't do this thing justice, so I pulled up a video chat and flipped the camera around to show the office.

"Why are you calling me from a warehouse?" Curtis asked when he answered. For the first time since we'd met, he was dressed casually in jeans and a t-shirt, brown hair tousled purposefully. He looked fresh and well-rested, as if unemployment agreed with him.

"Good question," I asked. "Did you by any chance know where your father was storing all the stuff he bought for his MLM?"

The color drained from Curtis's face as realization dawned. "He didn't."

"I'm afraid he did."

"Oh, man. I'm sorry, Lana," he said. "I'll talk to him. For now, call Scott in Maintenance and ask if they can put everything in storage for a few days. Let him know I'll take care of it as soon as I can."

As his father's Chief of Staff for several years, Curtis knew everything about this building and the people who worked in it. It didn't surprise me at all that he knew exactly who I could talk to about getting this resolved.

Too bad I couldn't ask him to show me around on my first day, since I wouldn't be here if he'd won the election. We'd become friendly, but not that friendly. Even though I thought, deep down, he looked forward to having some time to rest and relax and think about the next step in his life after always doing what his father expected. Something we had in common.

A phone call later, the maintenance staff came to help clear out my space. Even with four people and two dollies at our disposal, it took most of the morning. Turned out, the boxes extended beyond the welcome area into my office. Regular pole fitness classes kept me strong, but my pencil skirt wasn't designed for bending and lifting.

When we finished, Jason took a satisfied look around the inner office. "Much better! You have a reception desk. With a landline and a computer. Even a chair. See how well we treat our freshman senators?"

"Wow. I sure hope the special treatment doesn't go to my

head. All this, and my own personal senator to show me around."

"Well, that would be lovely, but I'm afraid I have to go soon," Jason said. "We'll talk more later, but one of the first things you should do is hire a Chief of Staff."

"Yeah, I have an idea about that, but if you have any recommendations, I'd appreciate it." Daniel O'Brien, the man who'd run my best friend's campaign and now her boyfriend, would probably step in and manage my staff for me if I asked him to. We'd had a couple of conversations about it. But since my term State Senator ended in January, he felt like he'd be more useful running my re-election campaign to keep me in place another two years.

We only had a few months to convince people that the write-in candidate who'd gotten a whopping fifteen votes should get a chance to serve a full term. I would do my best closer to November, but for now, I needed to find my footing. If I joined the Senate and immediately starting spending all my time running for re-election, even I wouldn't vote for me. The people of my district deserved better.

"I'll have my Chief of Staff email you later," he said. "I'm sure he can make some suggestions. You'll also need an assistant."

That, at least, was no problem. My current assistant had been with me since I started at my former law firm a few years ago. She'd become a surrogate mother, and I wouldn't even consider moving into a new position without her. She was spending today and tomorrow packing up my old files, reaching out to former clients, and transferring everything to the associate who'd be taking over all my cases. "Linda starts Wednesday."

"Okay, great. Looks like you're on top of things," Jason said. "I've got a meeting, but someone from IT should be here soon to get you set up in the system. Meanwhile, I brought some forms for you to fill out. Payroll and other HR stuff. If you need anything, please don't hesitate to reach out."

"I feel like you've done so much already."

"It's my job. Oh! Before I forget." He set another piece of paper atop the growing stack in my arms. "Here's a list of all the committees former Senator Baker served on."

"You want me to take all of his committee seats?" Butterflies reared up in my stomach at the thought of taking on so much on my first day.

He laughed. "No. Some have been filled. But take a look, see what you think. Some spots are open, and you could put your name in if you're interested. No one would expect you to sign up for more than one or two under the circumstances."

Because I was so new, or because everyone thought I was a stripper by association? It wasn't worth asking.

"Thanks so much," I said. "I guess I better get started."

"I'll be back around eleven-forty-five to take you to the cafeteria for lunch, if you want to join me?"

His words tempted me. It would be nice to eat with a friendly face. My dad was in the military, so we moved around a lot. I hated being the new kid, sitting alone in the cafeteria, surrounded by a sea of strangers. When Dad took early retirement and settled in Albany the summer before my junior year, it was the happiest day of my life. Unfortunately, for today, I'd made plans.

Disappointment tinged my voice. "Can I take a rain check? My parents are taking me to lunch to celebrate."

A lot of people would have made a snide comment about my parents taking me out to lunch at the age of twenty-seven, but I wasn't ashamed of having a close-knit family.

He smiled. "Of course. Text me, and we'll see what days I'm free. Maybe tomorrow."

"Sounds good." I watched him go with the slight pang that accompanied realizing I was suddenly on my own.

Ah, well. Not the first time I'd been a stranger in a new situation and look how far I'd come. Full of determination, I turned my attention to the mountain of paperwork needing my attention. As a trained lawyer, I couldn't even fill out the W-9 or the Direct Deposit Payment authorization forms without reading every word, so it might take a while.

Sitting back in my chair, I took a moment to appreciate that I was actually sitting in the State House, in my own office, working as a New York Senator. The room itself wasn't terribly impressive, and not much larger than where I sat working for my prior firm. Two tall, narrow windows on the wall behind my desk gave me plenty of natural light. The New York and United States flags stood in either corner, reminding me of the importance and history of this room and this position. To my right were bookcases I would delight in filling for as long as I managed to stay here. To my left, a door led to the outer office my administrative assistant and Chief of Staff would eventually share.

The top of my mahogany desk gleamed, bare except for the computer monitor. Soon enough, it would be awash with books, memos, papers, etc.. For now, one thing was missing. Reaching into my bag, I pulled out a gift from Mel. A picture frame containing a shot of the two of us on the day we graduated from high school. Our arms slung around each other, matching giant smiles on our faces. It was before Mel got her braces removed. We looked so young, so full of promise.

I pressed a switch on the back, and the image flipped. Another shot of the two of us, but this time at my first pole doubles performance. On the left, Mel gripped her pole with her arms spread wide. Her bent legs pointed behind her gracefully, and her head was thrown back. Long brown hair streamed out behind her. A beautiful show of strength. On the right, I hung upside-down with one knee gripping the pole and the other leg pointed behind me. The image never failed to bring a smile to my face, and I liked just knowing it was there, hidden behind the office-appropriate photograph. I pressed the switch again, bringing teenaged Mel and Lana to the forefront before setting the frame beside my monitor.

Perfect.

Chapter Two

Tuesday morning dawned cold but beautiful. The sun on my shoulders made me feel optimistic as I walked into the State House. I still couldn't believe I worked here. Here, making decisions that affected the lives of twenty million New Yorkers.

But first, coffee.

This afternoon, I'd been invited to attend various committee meetings—so many, in fact, I'd need a cloning device to attend them all. But a few of the options did sound interesting, and after studying the pending legislation, I'd have an idea where to focus my time.

At the moment, roughly two hundred bills floated around somewhere in the legislative process. The initial number seemed overwhelming, but I didn't need to read and understand two hundred bills all at once. For one thing, five of them had been passed before the special election and currently sat on Governor's Abbot desk, awaiting a signature.

When a member of the legislature first proposed a new law, the bill didn't go to a vote right away. First, it had to go through various committees. The process could be startlingly quick with important measures everyone wanted to pass right away, but usually it took weeks or even months. The vast majority of bills that got referred to committees remained there and never went to a floor vote. The term used was "died in committee." This was common when the Assembly or Senate didn't want to bring something to a vote for one reason or another. The record would simply show a bill being referred to committee, then no further action.

Once all the necessary committees discussed, amended, and voted on a bill, then the full Senate and Assembly each voted before passing the bill on to the governor. If Governor Abbot signed the bill, then it went on the books. Otherwise, she could veto, and we'd need a two-thirds majority to override. An override wasn't common these days. The Governor was a savvy lady who usually signed any bill that made it to her desk with a veto-proof majority. Governors typically didn't like being overridden.

Roughly half of the two hundred currently-pending bills had passed the Senate and were awaiting a vote in the Assembly. There was nothing to do on those unless the Assembly sent them back requesting amendments, so I quickly filed those to be read when I had more time. Or if they passed. It was good to know what we were working on, but none of those bills needed my immediate attention.

Of the remaining bills, fifteen were scheduled for various proceedings over the next few weeks. Those were the ones to start on. And each of them was about twenty pages between the bill summaries, the full text, the amendments, and the history of all action taken so far. Everything added up to a lot of very dense reading.

The bill summaries were an excellent place to start, but it didn't take me long to realize they'd been drafted by the person who sponsored the bill (well, by their Chief of Staff). Thus, according to the summaries, every potential law sounded like the most amazing idea anyone ever came up with.

After an hour, my eyes started to blur. I couldn't believe how far in over my head I'd found myself. My first instinct was to call Mel and ask her what the hashtag she'd been thinking, asking people to write in my name on the ballot.

My best friend had decided to run after she discovered the only candidate for an open seat was running on the "stop pole fitness" platform. But as the campaign went on, she realized politics didn't make her happy. When she and her opponent both had to drop out, they agreed to ask people to vote for me instead. Sometimes I wondered why I'd agreed. I'd only been a lawyer for a few years. As much as I appreciated my best friend's faith in me, and the idea of making a difference excited me a lot more than litigating worker's compensation claims, being an elected official terrified me.

What if I failed spectacularly? What if I wound up as much as a punchline as the man who'd occupied this office before me? The list of things that could go wrong was longer than the list of people who voted for me in the first place.

My phone beeped with a message, a welcome distraction.

Jason: How's day two going? Everything okay?

Me: I might be hallucinating from all this reading. Is someone really sponsoring a bill to eliminate minimum wage?

Jason: You sound surprised.

Me: I'm very impressed with whoever wrote this summary. I mean, "if there is no minimum wage, there can be no maximum! The sky is the limit for our workers."

Jason: Uh-oh. Sounds like you're in favor.

I shot back a series of emojis showing someone laughing until tears came out of their eyes. Then,

Me: This person's skills are wasted in the State House. They should be writing fantasy.

Jason: I'll let them know.

Jason: There's a meeting of the Racing, Gaming, and Wagering Committee starting in fifteen minutes. You want to join me?

Saratoga County was best known for our racetrack, so it came as no surprise to me that Senator Baker had been a member of the Racing, Gaming, and Wagering Committee. I wasn't positive I wanted his vacant seat, but I should know what items were being discussed. It truly was in my best interest to go and observe the meeting. Especially if Jason would be there. It would be nice to see a friendly face after a morning of drowning in legalese. And I liked legalese.

Me: I'm in. Where?

Five minutes later, I met Jason outside the door to the smaller room where committees held hearings. I still hadn't set foot in the full legislative chamber during a session (other than the time I observed during law school). Today he wore a navy suit that looked great against his golden skin with a pale blue shirt. The suit itself wasn't expensive, but well-made and tailored to fit. As someone who loved to sew, I appreciated the craftsmanship.

To my surprise, after leading me to a seat in the audience, Jason sat beside me. "Don't you need to sit with the rest of the committee?"

"Oh, I'm not a member."

I started to ask why we were here then, but the answer hit me immediately. He'd taken time out of his busy schedule to bring me to a committee hearing so I wouldn't have to attend by myself. He didn't have to be here, but he knew it would interest me and my constituents. The right thing to do would be to let him know I didn't need a babysitter and send him back to work, but I selfishly wanted to keep him with me for a few minutes.

"Thanks for doing this."

"It's my pleasure," he said. "I remember what it's like to be new and overwhelmed. I like helping others."

Before I could respond, the Committee Leader called the meeting to order. There appeared to be seven members, none of whom I had met so far. Several of them looked familiar from the website. There was Senator Applebee, who represented a neighboring community. That made sense. Anyone who served a district bordering Saratoga would also want to be here.

Out of the corner of my eye, I studied Jason's profile. He listened to the discussion with rapt attention. Since he didn't realize I was looking at him, my eyes were free to roam greedily over his features. Too bad he was a co-worker, my mentor. He was very good-looking, not to mention considerate enough to take time out of his day to bring me to a hearing he thought would benefit me. Two things I'd be looking for if I was interested in finding someone to date. Darn it.

The third item on the agenda dealt with the treatment of animals used in horse racing. Although I hadn't had time to familiarize myself with every proposed law before the committee, as a long-time Saratoga Springs resident, I had many feelings about the subject. There was a history, it was a tradition, the race track made a great brunch (and brought in loads of money to the area). However, there were a lot of issues with how the animals were treated. I knew all the arguments for and against, and I also knew trying to ban or radically change racing would be career suicide. Especially during my first week. The current bill didn't seem likely to make it out of the committee, which was unfortunate. Healthy horses benefitted the owners, the tourists, the patrons, everyone.

Before fully thinking about it, I lunged to my feet and raised my hand.

"The chair recognizes the woman in the second row. Your name, please?"

"Lana Chen, Mr. Chairman. I represent the people of Saratoga Springs."

"You took Tiberius Baker's seat?"

"Yes, sir."

"Well then, Senator Chen, it's nice to meet you," Senator Wolf said. "Did you have anything to add?"

"I just wanted to point out that one of the largest expenses for owners can be the cost of unexpected injuries. If we improve regulations so the animals are better cared for, wouldn't the owners become more profitable down the line?"

"You're assuming that taking care of the horses will prevent injury."

"Yes. It seems like a logical conclusion based on my research."

"Senator, did you recently join this committee without my knowledge?" Senator Wolf asked.

My cheeks grew warm. "No, sir. But you're discussing an area of great importance to my constituents. I have many thoughts on this matter."

"Congratulations." He slammed the gavel. "I nominate you to fill our vacant seat. Any objections?"

Oops. This wasn't my intent at all. I just thought they'd missed some important points in their discussion—it sounded like they were going to skip the whole thing without even talking about it. With no idea what to do, I glanced at Jason. His shoulders shook with silent laughter.

"Did you know this would happen?" I hissed through clenched teeth.

He wiped his eyes. "I swear I didn't, but it's awesome."

At the front of the room, the existing members of the committee unanimously voted me in. My mouth opened and closed soundlessly.

"Well, this has been an interesting morning," Senator Wolf said. "I move that we adjourn until tomorrow so Senator Chen can review our agenda and catch up. Senator, can you be prepared to argue these bills in detail tomorrow?"

Unable to speak, I simply nodded. I remained in place, frozen to the floor, as Senator Wolf adjourned the meeting. The committee members filed out. With no one else in the audience, soon enough, Jason and I found ourselves alone. He also hadn't moved.

I let out a moan and sank into my chair. "What just happened?"

"Well, for one thing, you made my week."

"I just—they weren't even discussing the bill! They were going to let it die without doing anything. The horses are the ones who do all the work. They deserve better treatment." I sighed. "I should get back to my office and figure out what I got myself into."

Jason stood and gestured for me to lead the way out of the room. "You know, the more time we spend together, the more I think you may be exactly what we need around here."

Funny. The more time I spent with him, the more I thought he might be exactly the ally I needed. I told him as much.

"This could be the beginning of a beautiful friendship," he said.

I grinned up at him. "You like old movies, too?"

"Guilty." His phone rang, and the smile slid off his face. "Sorry, I've got to take this. We'll catch up later, okay?"

"Definitely."

Moments after I settled behind my desk, the door to my office slammed open, bouncing off the wall. I leapt to my feet as a tall woman with long, swishy red hair stormed into my space. "I need to see Senator Baker immediately."

Fork me. Jason was right. I needed an assistant.

Chapter Three

W ell, this was awkward.

Clearing my throat, I pulled myself up to my full height, which brought me almost to this woman's shoulder. Despite having to look up several inches, I met her green eyes squarely. "Senator Baker resigned three months ago. I'm Senator Chen."

She huffed at me. "Yes, I'm aware of that. I'm looking for Senator *Curtis* Baker."

Just when I thought things couldn't get weirder. No one told me I'd taken a job in the Twilight Zone. Apparently this woman didn't read the news. Or her email. Surely someone had told the existing legislators I'd be joining them.

"As I said, I'm Senator Chen. How can I help you?"

Finally, she really looked at me. Her eyes swept from the top of my five-foot-two-inch frame over my perfectly tailored (by me) black pin-striped suit to my four-hundred-dollar heels before settling back on my face. Her expression left me no clue whether I'd passed her inspection. "Where's Curtis?"

"I'm afraid I don't have the faintest idea. Who are you?"

She ignored the question. "Hold up. You're not telling me Curtis lost the election, are you? You're the stripper?"

I wasn't in the mood to give a lecture on slut-shaming before even getting this woman's name, so I refused to take the bait. "Close. I'm a lawyer."

"I don't get it."

"What's the difference between a lawyer and a jellyfish?"

"I'm sure I have no idea."

"One's a spineless, poisonous blob. The other's a form of sea life." She continued to stare at me blankly, so I decided once again to try another tack. Holding out one hand, I said, "I'm Lana. And you are?"

"You don't know?" She shook her head while I pondered the politest way to tell her I typically didn't ask questions I knew the answer to. "Whatever. I'm Gretchen."

"You didn't know I won the election? All the local sites covered it. I was even trending on Twitter."

She shrugged. "I just got back from leave. I was here when old Tiberius walked out, and I assumed Curtis would take his seat. Everyone did."

It was on the tip of my tongue to ask if she'd bothered going to the polls on Election Day. Maybe I wouldn't be here if she had. It didn't matter, though, because here I was, occupying this office. "Right. I guess I assumed it would be big news when both candidates dropped out of the election the night before the polls opened and recommended that people vote for a write-in third party instead."

Her jaw dropped. "Is that what happened? No one even voted for you?"

I didn't have time to fall any further into this rabbit hole. If she wanted to know what happened, she could ask Google. "How can I help you, Gretchen?"

"I'm increasingly certain you can't."

"Great! It was nice to meet you." I held up a sheaf of

papers. "Well, not really, but I was trying to be polite. I've got a lot of reading to do, so if you don't mind, could you close my door on the way out?"

"You're going to tomorrow's hearings."

"Yes." My words weren't penetrating, but I didn't know how to be any clearer. For the third time, I said, "I'm the new. State. Senator. For. Saratoga Springs."

"I got it," she snapped. "I'm not an idiot. I'm surprised you'd jump into the fray so quickly when you have no idea what's going on."

I met her gaze unflinchingly. I still didn't get why she was trying to intimidate me, but I wouldn't let her efforts pay off. "I'm a quick learner."

"Yes, I hear strippers have many delightful talents," she said. My fingers itched to slap the smug expression off of her face. "Anyway, I work for Theo Rumsfeld."

The name sounded vaguely familiar. I racked my brain for a minute until it came to me. The longer I thought, the more disappointed in me Gretchen looked. But finally, my excessive love for Google came in handy. "Oh! He's the majority leader."

"Actually, he's the minority leader now, thanks to you. But yes. I'm his Chief of Staff."

Thanks to me. Yikes. I'd forgotten that, before Senator Baker retired, his party held a one-seat majority. Which had now tipped in the other direction. The evidence that Gretchen and I weren't about to become best friends kept mounting. And I still didn't know what she was doing in my office.

She evaluated me from head to toe as if deciding whether to purchase a prized horse. "I like your suit. Where did you get it?"

If this conversation got any weirder, I was going to get dizzy. Maybe this was her plan. But in the interest of being polite, I said, "Thank you. I made it."

"Seriously?"

"Yeah. I like to sew." It wasn't worth mentioning that, at my height, nothing fit off the rack. It was less annoying to make stuff when I could than to alter everything. She continued looking at me like she didn't understand why I stood in my own office. "Why were you looking for Curtis?"

"Because he would've known the answer."

Although I knew it behooved me to play nice, especially during my first week, I couldn't help the response that slipped out. "Gee, has anyone ever told you that you're utterly delightful?"

She tilted her head and narrowed her eyes at me. "No."

"Shocking." This conversation was shooting down the hill now. "Let's start over. I'm Lana Chen, freshly elected senator for Saratoga Springs and the surrounding areas."

"Right." She took a deep breath. "I'm sorry. Change flusters me, and I've been seeing a lot of it."

"Tell me about it," I said. "A week ago, I never thought I'd wind up here."

Her face moved into what might've been a smile. Or, you know, swallowing a sneeze. "The Minority Leader wanted me to help him find someone to cosponsor a new zoning bill with him. He's known Curtis for years. We thought listing them together might help raise Curtis's profile."

From what I'd heard of Rumsfeld, he never did anything without an ulterior motive, so I suspected there was more to the story. I also suspected that, knowing his politics, he wouldn't jump at the chance to have me co-author a bill with him instead.

"Zoning? What's it about?"

Before she could tell me, a knock sounded on the door frame. "Excuse me."

I turned to see the interloper. The man standing in my doorway could only be described as what Mel would call "ugly sexy." None of his features were conventionally attractive: nose a smidge too long, lips too thin, eyes on the beady side. His too-puffy hair was a nondescript shade of dishwater blonde. His ears stuck out, but not in a Will-Smith-sexy kind of way.

And yet, the overall effect? Completely hot. Maybe it was his silky smooth, almost melodic, voice. Or maybe it was the look of distaste he directed at the woman irritating me. "There you are, Gretchen. The Senator is looking for you."

She heaved a sigh and shook her head. "I told him… Sorry. Yes, of course. I'm on my way."

As soon as she left, he turned to me. "You're welcome."

"Um… thank you? What did you do?"

"I saved you from Gretchen."

Realization slowly dawned. "The Senator's not looking for her?"

"Who knows? I didn't say which Senator. I'm sure one of them wants to talk to her. The Minority Leader's a busy guy, and she handles a lot of his workload." He held out his hand. "I'm Steve."

"Lana Chen, newbie Senator." He had a firm handshake, smooth palms. His hand fit neatly into mine, making me feel secure.

"Whoa! You've got quite a grip there."

"I work out."

If he hadn't heard the rumors, no need to enlighten him. If he had heard the rumors…no need to enlighten him. I'd been elected to do a job (by fifteen votes!), and I'd do it. What I did in my free time wasn't relevant.

"Nice to meet you. What do you do around here? You're not a Senator."

"How do you know?"

"Because I spent hours on the state's website yesterday, researching every member of the Assembly and Senate. I'd have remembered you."

A slow smile spread across his face. Ugly sexy, yup. And

from the gleam in his eye, I suspected Steve knew how appealing I found him. "Me? I'm not interesting. Like you, work is my life. I've never even had time to see much of the area, other than the blocks from my hotel to downtown. I work to help pass legislation related to government affairs."

I rolled his description over in my mind for a minute. "You're a lobbyist?"

"Guilty," he said. "I'll understand if you want to throw me out of your office." He looked down at his left hand as if noticing for the first time he carried a large envelope. "But before you do, we've got some hearings coming up at the end of this week. Mostly routine stuff. I took the liberty of preparing a summary to get you up to speed."

"Thanks so much!" My first instinct was to be genuinely touched at his thoughtfulness. Then I realized that if these were bills he wanted to pass, he'd probably just printed the bill summaries, which would make each bill sound life-changing and amazing for everyone. At least if he were any good at his job.

"You're welcome. It's basic stuff. The kind of bills that'll wind up passing with ninety percent of the vote. We all show up, and everyone votes 'aye.' Still, it's good to look it over."

Duh. I wasn't about to rubber-stamp legislation without knowing anything about it. "I will, thanks."

"You're welcome. If you need anything—anything at all— please don't hesitate to ask." He handed me his card. Our fingers brushed, and a jolt of lightning went through me. Steve's eyes locked with mine, and suddenly I didn't want him to leave my office. "Are you free for lunch? I could show you around, give you the lay of the land."

When he said "lay of the land," my mind instantly went to something very different from showing me where to find the cafeteria. Not his fault, mine. And it was tempting. He had broad shoulders, wasn't too tall, looked like he knew how to show a girl a good time. But I wasn't here for dating. And neither was he, presumably.

Jason had mentioned something about lunch one day this week, but we hadn't made a firm plan. He was a busy guy, so I shouldn't assume he was available today. No reason for me to take up any more of his time. After all, the poor guy spent half of yesterday morning moving boxes out of my office. Way above and beyond the duties of meeting a new senator.

"Sounds great!" I said, moving around my desk and picking up my purse.

The legislature's cafeteria looked like what I expected from having watched about four hundred million legal shows and movies. The food also wasn't terribly exciting, but it was food. I wasn't here to eat, anyway. I was here to see and be seen, to meet my fellow legislators before sitting in on more committee hearings, and to get to know Steve.

Also to pick his brain, because it occurred to me that he might be able to answer some questions for me.

"Hey, how well do you know Gretchen?"

He shrugged. "She's highly efficient, great at juggling schedules, and has the personality of chewing aluminum foil."

I laughed at the all-too-accurate comparison. "And Rumsfeld's been around forever, right?"

"I think he was first elected around the time I started high school," he said. "Why?"

"Just curious. She said she thought Curtis won the special election, which makes no sense. And she apparently wanted him to cosponsor some bill? To be honest, I have my doubts. Something's weird."

He shrugged. "She was out last week, so it's possible she missed the news. Surprising, but maybe she's had a lot going on. As for the bill, Rumsfeld never does anything controversial. It's why his voters love him. It was probably something exciting like a campaign suggesting we remind people to wear seatbelts."

"Yeah, maybe." Something still bugged me, but then I spotted Jason across the room. When I waved, he smiled and started toward me. Then his gaze landed on Steve, and his face shuttered closed. Uh-oh.

I'd only been here less than two days, and I was already making mistakes. Wonderful.

Chapter Four

The look on Jason's face when he spotted me with Steve made me queasy. It never occurred to me to ask if there were certain people I should avoid. Suddenly, I wondered if the internal politics of the Senate were like high school. What if I'd accidentally sat at the cool kids' table. Was I not allowed to eat with a lobbyist? It's not like he was going to brainwash me in the middle of the cafeteria in front of everyone.

As Jason approached, I wiped my palms on my skirt and steeled myself for a lecture. We were just getting lunch. It's not like I was telling Steve any state secrets. I didn't even know any state secrets yet, and to be honest, if I did, I was smart enough not to share them in a public lunchroom.

A deep breath cleared my mind a little, but I couldn't shed my nervousness as my mentor approached the table. I hated the thought of upsetting him on my first day.

"Hey, Lana," Jason said when he reached the table. "Everything okay? I thought we were having lunch."

"Were we?" I wrinkled my brow, trying to recall the conversation. "I'm sorry. I thought you were going to text me about 'one day this week.'"

"My misunderstanding, then." A flicker of disappointment flashed in his eyes.

I turned to Steve. "Turns out, Jason is a hands-on mentor. He spent over an hour helping me move boxes out of my office when I got here."

"Huh."

"All in a day's work." Jason grinned at me before he turned to Steve and cleared his throat. From the way Steve stiffened, it was clear they weren't friends. "I didn't realize you two knew each other."

"I rescued her from Gretchen earlier," Steve said. "Lana agreed to accompany me to lunch as a thank you."

"Huh. I thought you and Gretchen were friends," Jason said. "You certainly seem chatty."

Steve shook his head. "No way, man. It's my job to get along with everyone."

When Jason offered to meet me for lunch, I'd thought he was being polite. But he appeared to be alone. Suddenly I wondered if I offended him by eating with someone else. Someone who, unless I missed my guess, he didn't like at all. "Do you want to join us?"

"No, thank you," he said. "I just spotted Senator Clamurro. We have some things to discuss before this afternoon's Finance Committee meeting."

"Finance Committee, huh? Exciting stuff."

"Watch it," he said. "Talk like that will get you drafted to join us. We have an opening now."

I shuddered. "I take it all back."

"So he's your mentor?" Steve asked after Jason walked away. "I'm sorry."

Something about his tone took me aback. "Why are you sorry? He helped me a lot yesterday. I'm looking forward to working with him."

Steve's cheeks tinged red. "I shouldn't have said anything. You may have noticed that we're not bosom buddies."

"Yeah, I got the sense he doesn't like you." I picked up a French fry. "Is there some juicy legislative gossip I should know about?"

"Hardly. It's not an interesting story."

"Come on, bore me."

Steve shrugged. "A while back, we liked the same girl. She went out with me instead of him. Things didn't work out between us, but he never forgave me."

"What a shame."

"It's no big. I barely knew the guy before it happened." He took a bite of his hamburger. "Anyway, enough drama. Tell me about yourself. What brings you here?"

"Fifteen write-in votes," I said proudly. "Turns out, it's not unheard of. In 2005, a man won the mayorship with a write-in campaign after he netted twenty-nine votes. Apparently his opponent thought he had the election in the bag and didn't campaign."

He blinked at me. "I'm not sure whether I should be impressed you know that off the top of your head or terrified by your enormous brainpower."

I laughed. "I looked it up on my phone while waiting for the IT department to grant me access to my computer yesterday morning. Google is your friend."

"True," he said. "But that's not what I want to know. Tell me about the path Lana Chen was on before she became the first senate write-in candidate anyone can remember."

"Okay, but if you fall asleep and hit your head on the table, it's not my fault."

"I'll take my chances." If he kept smiling at me like that, I was going to forget my name. Steve wasn't the kind of guy I normally went for, but he definitely had a certain appeal.

Something in the way he carried himself or our easy rapport made me want to keep talking to him.

"Okay, then," I said. "My dad was in the Air Force, my mom a nurse. They met when they were both stationed in Germany. She worked at the base hospital. We moved around a lot when I was younger. When I was fourteen, Mom's mom got sick. She wanted to move home to be close to them. Dad took early retirement and got a pilot job at the local airport. Nonna got better, but we stayed."

"Why?"

I shrugged. "I was in high school, settled for the first time in my life. Mom liked being near her parents. Dad had a good job he enjoyed. We didn't have any reason to leave."

"I guess that makes sense."

"Anyway, I went to college in New Haven, Connecticut, but came home for law school. I didn't want to be away from my family for another three years."

"What made you go into law?"

"I didn't have a clear goal for my future. Everyone said with a law degree you can do anything. Of course, because of that, everyone has a law degree now. But I sort of fell into a job with a worker's compensation firm, and now I'm here."

"You 'fell into' worker's comp, huh? Did you sue?"

"Heh." Our eyes met across the table, and my heart fluttered. "Luckily, I wasn't injured. Anyway, while I liked helping people get what they were owed, the job wasn't for me."

"Why not?"

"It didn't excite me. I worked long hours, I paid the bills. Not a lot of time for anything but work. It always seemed like there should be more to life," I said. "My best friend Mel was trying to help me figure out what I wanted to do when this came up. To be honest, I didn't think anyone would vote for me."

"But they did."

"Yeah, a whopping fifteen people. Including Mel, her campaign manager Daniel, and Curtis. The rest must've been reporters who were at one of the press conferences. I didn't even vote."

"Don't forget your parents."

"I didn't." My lips twitched at the revelation. "They voted for Mel."

He let out a fake gasp. "They didn't!"

"Cross my heart. They don't watch the news, and they wake up early in the morning. They had no idea she and Curtis both dropped out until I talked to them later. By then, they'd voted."

"Imagine how embarrassing it would've been if you'd lost solely because of your parents."

"Well, the good news is, no one would have remembered after about a week. The only reason I'm interesting at all is because no one expected me to be here."

"That's not the only reason. Personally, I find you fascinating." He cleared his throat. "I mean, um, I'm glad you're here."

"Thanks. Me, too." As much as I'd doubted Mel's plan, I'd been thrilled when it worked. Over the weeks of her campaign, I enjoyed doing research and helping out as I could. I'd accompanied Mel to multiple events and learned a lot about what went on behind the scenes in politics. I loved all of it. At one point when it looked like she might win, I'd even been a little jealous. Not that I'd told Mel. I didn't need to, though. She knew me better than anyone in the world.

Secret fact: I did write in my name. I wanted to be a state senator, even if I hadn't run. To be fair, though, I did that regularly. A search of the state's voting archives would show "Lana Chen" as receiving at least one write-in vote in every election dating back for years, for positions from District Attorney to County Medical Examiner.

In my defense, no one told me they kept records of those things. I couldn't bring myself to vote for some of the people who ran unopposed. Then one day I was googling myself and I saw all the random votes for me here and there, always in the same county. Oops.

Our conversation made me realize that I somehow found myself working yet another job I didn't think about or pursue. It came along, and I grabbed it. It sounded interesting, and I wasn't loving my old job. Daniel filed the papers to run for re-election right away because there was no time to think before they were due. If I won, then I'd have a whole two-year term to decide my next step. But would I make a decision? Or would I float along, looking for something else to grab onto?

The longer Steve and I chatted, the more I realized I'd never had a plan for my life. I went to college because it was expected, law school because I didn't know what else to do, and then I'd literally taken the only two jobs that came up. Wow. Suddenly very uncomfortable, I was about to change the subject when Steve leaned forward and lowered his voice.

"Is that why you did the stripper thing? To pay for law school?"

Oh, man. Not him, too. I refused to dignify his comment with a response. Instead, I took a large bite of my burger and chewed it thoughtfully. The silence stretched out, but I refused to break it.

Finally, his face turned red. "I'm sorry. I was out of line. Forget I asked."

"Done," I said after swallowing. "So, lobbying, huh? Sounds interesting."

"It can be. And sometimes I find out there's another group trying to reinstate Prohibition."

"At least you know it'll never pass. Why do they even bother?"

He shrugged. "It happens every few years."

"Seriously? That's so bizarre."

"Yeah. Feeling like you're living in a warped version of *Footloose* gets old after a while. Anyway, I grew up in New York City. Went to Columbia, got my law degree there, and now here I am, fighting the good fight."

"So you're a city boy, huh?"

"Yes, I am," he said proudly. "New York is the best city in the world. Go, Yankees!"

"You like the Yankees? Sorry, I'm not much of a basketball fan."

The look on his face nearly made me burst out laughing, but somehow I held it together. "Lana, I thought we were becoming friends."

"What?" I widened my eyes innocently. "Oh, I get it. The Yankees don't play basketball. I'm afraid I'm not big on football either."

"You're breaking my heart." Steve clutched his chest and sighed so dramatically, I burst out laughing.

"Oh, man. You should've seen the look on your face."

"That's not funny!" He shook his head, lips twitching. "Okay, it was a little funny. At least you're not a Mets fan."

"To be honest, I'm really not into sports, although I know the major teams around here. And I've never been to New York City, so I have no opinion on Mets versus Yankees."

Steve choked on his burger. After a long coughing fit, he leaned back in his chair and gazed at me. "Tell me you're messing with me again."

I raised my hand to my heart. "Scout's honor."

"Hold on," he said. "What do you mean you've never been to New York? You said you've been living in the Capital District for more than ten years."

"Not to put too fine a point on it, but we're *in* New York now. There is more to the state than the city."

"If you say so." He rolled his eyes. "I'll rephrase. Are you telling me you've never been to *New York City*? Statue of Liberty, Central Park? The Met? Broadway?"

"Guilty," I said sheepishly. "Most of my free time in high school was spent with my grandparents since Nonna was sick. Then I had college and law school, and…it never seemed to happen."

"Your dad's a pilot. Seriously, you couldn't fly down to the City for a weekend? That's sad, Lana."

"My dad's a pilot. Why would we go to New York for the weekend when we could go to Paris?"

"I guess you've got me there," he said. "Except New York is a million times better than Paris."

"We'll have to agree to disagree," I said. "Besides, you said you've never taken in the local sights of Albany. What's your excuse? You've worked here almost a decade."

"Don't change the subject. This is about your tragic lack of experience, not mine."

"You *work* here. The legislature is in session for several months each year. You get paid to spend time in Albany, and presumably, you sleep here. You mentioned a hotel—You don't commute from New York City, right?"

"No. I travel all over the state. I'm usually in Albany two or three days a week, but I go home for the weekend when I can."

"It's weirder that you've never seen the local sights. I've never had a reason to go to New York City."

"Well you do now," he said. "Come on. You've got to go with me."

"I'll make a deal with you," I said. "You let me show you around the Capital District, introduce you to our local history, and I'll visit any place you want in the City."

"Only if you let me take you." He held out one hand. His palm felt pleasantly warm against mine. "There's nothing like getting a tour of the City from a native."

Despite already being so busy I wasn't sure when I'd find a

free minute, the thought of spending time with Steve outside work sent a little thrill through me. Besides, I'd been thinking about needing to make more time for fun. Wasn't that my reason for leaving my old job?

I put my hand out to shake. "Deal."

Chapter Five

After work, I stopped to pick up takeout and hightailed it straight to Mel's condo. Normally after a grueling day at the office, I'd hit up her studio for a class, but she'd decided not to go back to Dance 4U after the owner fired her for no reason. Really, who could blame her?

Until she signed a lease for a new studio, all of our lessons were one-on-one, either at her place or mine. We each had a fitness pole installed in our living rooms. Which, come to think of it, would do nothing to dispel the stripper rumors if anyone from the legislative offices saw it. I made a mental note to take the pole down before inviting anyone from work over. It worked as a tension rod, easy enough to put back up whenever I wanted. It also came apart easily for storage.

Mel met me at the door, eyeing the plastic bags bursting with food in my hands. "Rough first week?"

"I object to the question on the grounds that you're trying to get me to break my no-swearing pact." Moving past her, I went straight to the kitchen and started unpacking containers: two dozen buffalo wings, salad, two large calzones, mozzarella sticks, and lava cakes for dessert. "Actually, not bad. Just a bit overwhelming."

Okay, it *was* a lot of food. But venting burned calories, and so did pole fitness. Both of which I planned to do for the next few hours.

"This is all your fault, you know."

"Guilty," Mel said unabashedly. She didn't even have the courtesy to blush. "But I also know you're going to kick butt at this job. You weren't happy where you were, and the people of New York are lucky to have someone like you working to make our state even better."

Her words brought an unexpected smile to my face. "You know it's impossible for me to be mad at you when you talk to me like that."

"Yes." She hugged me before picking up a paper plate and starting to serve herself. "But it's all true. I would've done the job, but I'd have been calling you every day to beg for help."

"Funny you should mention that." After settling into my stool, I filled her in on the day's events around mouthfuls of delicious fried food. When I got to the part about Gretchen, she snorted.

"Wow. Who does she think she is?"

I shrugged. "There's no way she didn't know who I am. It's not believable. She works for the prior majority leader. He's been minority leader for like three days because of me. There's no way his top aide doesn't know."

"Why lie about it? Does she want to see if you'll bite?"

"No clue. She must have some reason for trying to make me feel unimportant. Won't work, though. I'm the swing vote, and I know it."

Mel raised her hands over her head and clasped them together as if raising a sword. "You have the power!"

"Thanks, He-Man." I giggled. "It's not all bad. Jason's nice, and I'm excited to sit on the Racing, Gaming, and Wagering Committee, even if my getting seated wasn't intentional. Lunch with Steve was good."

"Judging by the smile on your face, I'd say it was more than 'good.' Are you smitten with a co-worker before you've even been there a week? Did I teach you nothing?"

"Based on how your 'forbidden relationship' worked out, I'd say you have no room to talk." During her campaign, Mel had been surprised to find herself falling for her campaign manager. They'd fought their feelings admirably to avoid hurting Mel's image with the voters, but the moment she threw in the towel, they stopped pretending. "Speaking of, how are things with Daniel?"

Her entire face lit up at the mere mention of his name. "Good. Wonderful."

"You still making him pole?"

"You know it," she said. "He's a natural. Don't tell him, but I'll have him doing doubles with me by fall."

I put my hands on my hips. "You wouldn't! What about me?"

She blew me a kiss. "You will always be my first and best doubles partner. But sometimes a girl wants to dance with someone who can toss her up in the air."

That I could not do, and it wasn't worth pretending. Not when it was time to dance.

Wheeling around on my stool, I went into Mel's bathroom to change into the workout clothes I'd brought with me. Nothing helped me ease work-related stress like some strength-based moves, and I'd taken several beatings already. From the sea of boxes in my office to Gretchen's utter dismissal of me as a person to multiple people making stripper comments, I needed an escape.

At my insistence, Mel led me through a grueling warm-up.

After about the hundredth fire hydrant lift on my left side, I forgot why I was so annoyed. By the time I finished my right leg, I barely knew my own name. Exactly what I needed.

"Forgive me for asking a silly question," she asked as she watched me lunge back and forth across the room for at least the fiftieth time, "but would you be interested in teaching a pole calisthenics class?"

My snort of laughter made me lose my balance. "Thanks, but I'll take a hard pass on you getting me any more jobs."

"Don't be ridiculous. You're going to rock this."

"Speaking of rocking things," I said, "how's the search for a space going?"

Mel had run for office in the first place after she lost her job. She'd looked briefly for a teaching job at another studio in the area, but she'd eventually realized her dream was to be self-employed. We'd been looking for a space for her to rent ever since she dropped out of the race, but these things took time.

Her face fell. "Not good, I'm afraid. I found the most amazing location, but it's not going to happen."

"Excuse me? Where's the I-Can-Do-Anything Mel we all know and love? The woman who ran for public office because the only candidate—who had decades of experience in politics—pissed her off?"

"That Mel lost," she pointed out.

"I'm not so sure about that," I said. "You kept Curtis out of the state senate. You helped him find his inner White Hat, and he's a million times happier now. You freed me from a job I hated. Plus, you're able to do anything you want because I'm obviously not going to pass laws to limit your freedom of expression."

"A long time ago, a wise woman told me never to get into a bar debate with a lawyer unless she was very, very drunk." Mel went to the fridge. "Want some wine?"

I laughed but accepted the glass. "I'm going to assume that means you've realized I'm right. But you're changing the subject. What's wrong with the space?"

She sat on the barstool beside me. "Nothing. It's perfect. High ceilings, enormous windows overlooking this gorgeous park. Plenty of parking in the nearby park, but also a private lot behind. It was a ballet studio, so the wall is already lined with mirrors. And unlike my last place, it's got weatherproofed windows. No more freezing all winter and sweltering all summer."

"Sounds perfect. What's the catch?"

"See for yourself." She flipped open her tablet and pulled up the photos. "These are the pictures from my tour earlier."

Immediately, I saw the problem. "Did you forget to tell me you also want to offer inside swim lessons?"

As Mel said, the empty studio had high ceilings, huge floor-to-ceiling windows on the outside wall, and plenty of mirrors everywhere else. A barre ran along one of the shorter walls, which would be cool for warming up and stretching if she kept it. A well-lit, cozy reception area would welcome new and returning students.

And about two feet of water covered every inch of the floor.

"I wish." She sighed. "The last tenant filed for bankruptcy and moved out of state, turning off the heat before they left. In January. The landlord told me they'd rather leave the place empty as a tax write-off than pay to fix it up. So if I want the space, I'm pouring a lot of money into it. Money I'd intended to use to pay my expenses while waiting for the business to turn a profit."

"Ouch. How much?"

She gave a number, and I choked on my wine. Opening a new business always required some output of capital, but the landlord was asking for more than twice the renovation budget we'd discussed. Considering she'd also need to pay for the fitness poles, professional installation, crash mats, a computer system, phones, a website, and everything else, paying to put floors in the studio could easily put the entire dream out of reach.

"There's no other option?"

"Every other place I've seen has bigger problems, believe it or not. Or at least more difficult to fix. Like being an hour away, or not allowing me to screw the poles into the floor and ceilings." Considering that an unattached pole could fall and seriously injure the user, leaving them unsecured wasn't an option. Even if Mel were willing—and I'd strongly advise against it—she'd never get insurance. "Oh, and the place that didn't have a bathroom and wouldn't let me add one. They said our students could use the place next door, which would be awesome for the advanced students who dance in their underwear."

Her words made me mourn the loss of her dream. She deserved for the studio to be a reality. What she needed was a partner, someone to put up the money but let her run the place as she saw fit. Suddenly, the solution seemed obvious.

I relished the chance to help my best friend achieve a life-long dream. She deserved this. After working so many hours for so long, I had plenty of cash in my savings. At the same time, I had no idea how to run a pole fitness studio and no desire to learn. With a silent partner, Mel could do whatever she wanted.

I loved being the one with both the means and opportunity to help the person who'd done so much for me over the years. "Get this place. You love it. I'll give you the money."

"I appreciate that, Lana, I do. But I'd feel terrible if I couldn't pay you back right away."

Although I hadn't been talking about a loan, she might be

more open to my proposal after we went over her other options. So I asked, "What about your parents?"

She shook her head. "I talked to Mom, but their retirement accounts aren't doing great. Besides, it's the same thing. I can't take money I might not be able to pay back."

"Fine. I can be a silent investor." As soon as the words were out of my mouth, I heard myself earlier, telling Steve I'd only ever fallen into jobs, without thinking about what I truly wanted. I firmly quashed the voice, though. This wasn't the same. I wanted to help Mel succeed. She was the one who would be doing the job, not me. I'd just be collecting some of the profits. "It wouldn't be a loan. I'll give you the money, you pay me twenty percent of the profits. Investments aren't loans, so if you don't make money, you don't have to pay me anything."

"You want to put your money into a pole fitness studio?" Mel's lips twitched. "Isn't it a little early to torpedo your chances of re-election?"

I snorted. "Curtis won't run again. He told me he's going camping for the next month. Some site up in the Adirondacks with no cell signal where his dad used to take the family as kids."

"Sounds lovely."

"Sure. Except for the dirt and bugs and freezing nights and lack of Google, sounds fab."

"Remind me not to invite you next time I go camping."

"You can't go camping; you're opening up a pole studio."

"Nice redirection, Counselor."

"Thank you!" I beamed at her. "Sure, someone could run against me in the fall. But who's going to be looking at my investments? I'm nobody. Now stop deflecting. What's the real problem? Are you worried that once you find an investor, you have to actually take a chance and do this?"

"Never do business with family or friends," she said. "Especially not friends who know you better than you know yourself."

Leaning over, I put one arm around her. She rested her head on my shoulder. "Mel. You can do this. You're a kick-butt pole fitness instructor. You're smart. You're savvy. You've got the personality and the drive to bring in the business. Also, let's be honest—loads of people will want to take a class from The Fall Girl."

She winced at the nickname she'd unintentionally earned during the debacle that dropped us into a life of politics. "If I agree, will you promise never to use that name again?"

"Deal. A verbal contract is legally binding in the state of New York."

"You're right," she said. "I'm scared. I'm scared I'm going to fail."

"That's absolutely understandable. I get it. But tell me something. What happens if you open a studio, and it goes out of business? Realistically."

She took a deep breath and ticked off the answer on her fingers. "I can't pay my mortgage. This place goes into foreclosure, and I move in with my best friend Lana."

I ignored her effort to bait me. "Okay. And what happens if you don't open the studio? Worst case."

Mel met my eyes, knowing I'd won. "I get a job in fast food. I can't pay my mortgage. This place goes into foreclosure, and I move in with you."

"Then what do you have to lose?"

"Nothing."

"And what do you have to gain?"

"Everything." She thought for a moment. "But if you're putting up the money, I want you to be a full partner. Fifty-fifty."

"Forty-nine, fifty-one," I said. She started to protest, but I held up one hand. "You need to be able to make decisions, especially when the Senate is in session and I'm unreachable for hours at a time. I know the law, but you know the business."

"Deal." Mel squealed, launching herself into my arms. "Let's do this."

Just like that, Push and Pole Fitness was born.

Chapter Six

The next morning found me once again neck-deep in paperwork, this time reviewing recommendations for my open Chief of Staff position. A Senator's Chief of Staff is their top political advisor and often helps at some stage of drafting legislation—looking for typos, if nothing else. This person needed to have a firm grasp on policy, excellent communication skills, great grammar, and a drive to make the world a better place. Ideally, they would agree with me on most policy issues, because I didn't want to spend all my time debating with my employees. At the same time, it would be good to have someone who could see all sides of an issue, help me consider points of view I hadn't thought about, if only so I would know how to counter any arguments that came up. Even though I wasn't planning to draft any major bills in the immediate future, I'd need help eventually. The goal was to hire someone who would be with me for a while (assuming I won re-election).

Maybe I watched too much *The West Wing*, but I liked the idea of being in my sixties and having my best friend working as my Chief of Staff. Too bad Mel wasn't interested.

On top of all their other duties, the Chief of Staff runs the Senator's office. Whoever I hired would report directly to me and oversee any other staff I hired.

When Daniel called to tell me I'd been elected, I'd initially asked Linda to be my Chief of Staff, but she insisted that the job required someone with more experience—and interest—in politics. She was a people person, perfectly happy to answer phones and greet my visitors and never, ever have to make any policy decisions about anything. She'd heaved a massive sigh of relief when I told her she could keep doing her old job in the new office.

As long as I managed to focus on the applications. So. Many. Applications. Hundreds of people wanted to work for me. Then again, unemployment was high, so many of these resumes likely had nothing to do with me personally.

After about an hour of reading, I remembered Jason's offer to make some recommendations. If he knew qualified people, it might help me narrow things down. Immediately, I messaged him. He replied a few minutes later, promising to send over a list of potential candidates.

Jason: Do you want me to have Billy email them to set up an initial screening interview?

Billy was his assistant, who had more than enough of his own work to do. I appreciated the offer, but I wanted to review everything and decide on my own whether to invite each potential candidate to apply.

Me: Thanks, but that's not necessary. If anyone looks like a good fit, I'll have Linda email them to set something up.

Jason: Sure thing. By the way, how do you feel about my cashing in that rain check for lunch?

Part of me had been hoping Steve would drop by and offer to eat lunch with me again, but after yesterday, I realized Jason hadn't offered solely to be polite. I think I hurt his feelings by eating with Steve instead of him. The last thing I wanted was to alienate the first person who'd gone out of his way to be nice to me. Especially when he was genuinely nice. I enjoyed talking to him, and I'd done enough research on his voting history to respect his opinions.

Me: Sounds great. We can talk more about my shortlist (assuming I finish making one).

Setting my phone aside without waiting for an answer, I went back to the mountain of submissions. How did so many people even know about the job in less than a week? Where did Daniel post it, Tinder? Each person seemed more qualified than the last, and to be honest, most of them sounded more qualified to be Senator than Chief of Staff. They all had better resumes than I did. At one point I considered hiring someone who admitted to having no relevant experience, just so I wouldn't feel like the most clueless person in the office. But they misspelled "Democrat" in an unfortunate manner that had me quickly hitting the delete button. I needed a Chief of Staff who wouldn't accidentally talk about feces.

Once I had fifteen people in the "maybe" pile and at least another two dozen applications to review, I decided to take a break and vet my potentials on social media. To start, I wanted someone smart enough to make their profiles private. After that, we'd see.

The intelligent "someone" I sought would not be Eddie Johnson. First, his profile pic was an extreme close-up of a guy in a speedo. More than I wanted to see of anyone who might work for me. But as I scrolled through his page, a recent status caught my eye.

Applied for a job working for the new stripper senator. Should make things interesting.

The words blurred together as fury gripped me. Oh, no. This was not good at all. His comment had two hundred and forty reactions, plus seventy-seven comments. I had no interest in reading them, but one reply near the top caught my eye.

How does making pizza qualify you for Senate Chief of Staff?

Making pizza? Eddie's resume was still open on my screen, so I clicked over and scanned it again. According to this, he'd earned a bachelor's degree in political science from Harvard and worked as a volunteer on multiple campaigns, including the 2020 Presidential Primary. He wasn't much older than me, but his interest in politics went back to high school. Everything looked great. Except, you know, Eddie's Facebook page, where the comments made it very clear that not a word on his resume was true. Maybe his name, if I wanted to give him the benefit of the doubt.

On a whim, I copied the first paragraph of his cover letter and pasted it into Google. Three seconds later, I found myself staring at a website titled "So you want to work in politics?" For a mere nineteen dollars and ninety-nine cents, I discovered, anyone could buy themselves a resume aimed at helping them get a job as a staffer. For an extra nine-ninety-nine, this company would generously add a cover letter. What a bargain! The "deluxe" package even included fake letters of recommendation for an additional fee. The longer I looked at the page, the more ill I became.

My first instinct was to punch in my credit card number and see what they sent me, but there was no point. The results were sitting on my screen, staring me in the face.

Before I did anything else, I fired off an email asking Daniel to take down the job listing, telling him I only wanted to hire a personal referral. He replied immediately in the affirmative, but didn't ask why. I wondered if he might have suspected something like this would happen. I didn't know how to ask. It didn't matter. Daniel wasn't the reason I got a bunch of crank applications. Part of me wanted to comment on Eddie Johnson's public status to tell him how he'd shot himself in the foot, but I decided to leave his hubris on display for any other potential future employers.

Going back to the multitude of applications, I read everything again, this time using a more critical eye. The same themes kept showing up over and over. The same wording in the cover letters, which I'd initially only skimmed in my hurry to get to the "meat" of the applications.

In my naiveté, I'd seen similar qualifications on multiple resumes and assumed people tended to follow the same general career path to get to this level. Maybe they did, but none of those people appeared to be in my stack of resumes. Most of these candidates appeared to have used the same website. Finding a Chief of Staff was going to be even more difficult than I'd thought.

By the time Jason arrived to take me to lunch, my head was swimming with all the information. I welcomed the chance to get up from my desk and take a walk, even if we were only going to the cafeteria down the hall. Sitting at my desk all day, boning up on what I needed to know before I started attending hearings, was giving me cabin fever. Maybe doing lunges around the building a few times after we ate would make me feel better.

"Hey, I have a question," I said as we passed the office across from mine. "What can you tell me about Minority Leader Rumsfeld? Is he a stand-up guy? I met Gretchen yesterday morning. She was very cagy about what she wanted from me. And also, she claimed she thought Curtis won the election, which makes no sense."

Jason snorted. "Rumsfeld? He's so crooked, he can't even lie in bed straight. That man's never done anything without an ulterior motive. If Gretchen is knocking on your door, you can bet they want something from you."

"That's what I thought. Thanks for the confirmation."

"You've got strong instincts. Don't doubt yourself." He paused. "What do your instincts tell you about Steve?"

"Lobbyist Steve?" I shrugged. "He seems nice."

"Is that all?"

I glanced at him warily, but he met my gaze without flinching. "Why does it matter?"

"I noticed the two of you seemed to be having a grand time at lunch. I never realized he was so funny."

After hearing Steve's story, I supposed Jason wouldn't find funny. It wasn't terribly amusing when the person you liked went out with someone else. But it was years ago. Why should Jason care if Steve and I shared a laugh over a burger?

"Is that a problem? Should Senators and lobbyists not be friendly?"

"Not too friendly, no." He paused. "Look, be careful. You're new, you don't know the ropes yet, and Steve's got a reputation."

"Oh yeah? What a coincidence. So do I." Too bad the entire building didn't think Steve was a stripper. Things could get interesting. Maybe I'd get Mel to teach us a pole doubles routine. The image of the two of us dancing together brought a smile to my face, which abruptly faded when I realized Jason was staring at me. "Look, I appreciate your concern, but I can take care of myself."

He started to say something, but stopped and shook his head. "Right. You're a grown woman. You don't need my help. I don't want him to take advantage of you."

"Thanks." Who did he think he was, my dad? This conversation was getting weird, so I changed the subject. I told him all about Eddie Johnson, explaining that the search for a new Chief of Staff might take a little longer than originally expected.

By the time I finished, he was laughing. "I'm sorry. It's not funny. But, I promise you, this is the most interesting thing to happen around here in a long time."

"Let's make it even funnier," I said. "I'll hire one of them. Pick someone at random. Do we have a dartboard? Who knows, maybe a political background is overrated and the pizza delivery guy is truly the best person to run my office."

"You know, if you really wanted to go that route…" He hesitated, as if reconsidering what he was about to say. "Don't hate me for suggesting this, but, well, Curtis was an excellent Chief of Staff."

"Curtis Baker? My best friend's former opponent who is also fifty percent of the reason I'm here?"

Jason flushed. "I assumed you would hate the idea, but hear me out. First, you know he didn't believe any of the garbage he was spewing during the campaign. He was trying to be what he thought the people wanted to get the job."

"Fair enough, but I'm not sure 'changes positions to benefit himself' is what I'm looking at in a Chief of Staff, either."

"What about 'can argue any issue from both sides'? Because that's something you need to be able to do before you can change positions." He took a bite of his cheeseburger and chewed it thoroughly. "It was just an idea. He might help you out, at least temporarily. Besides, aren't you friends now? You didn't hesitate before calling him about the boxes yesterday."

"We're friendly acquaintances. Calling us friends might be straining the truth." I pushed my food away, too full of nervous energy to enjoy it. "He's the reason I'm here. And I like the guy, we'd work well together. And… Wait. I get it. You want me to bring him in to give me some street cred with the Old Timers."

"Guilty," he said sheepishly. "It's good for new Senators to show a willingness to reach across the aisle. Hiring a former opponent can help raise their respect for you. But also, you're in a precarious position. You're a completely unknown commodity, and you joined us after a sensational election season. Bringing in someone familiar might be comforting. For everyone, really. Wouldn't you like to have another friend around here?"

I really didn't want to comfort the old guard. One of the reasons I'd leapt at this opportunity was the ability to shake things up, make a change. But I did need someone competent. Bonus if we got along. I did like Curtis, a realization that startled me once I got to know him.

Suddenly hungry again, I pulled my plate toward me. "I'll think about it."

Chapter Seven

The search for a Chief of Staff dragged on. I preferred not to work with Curtis, but wasn't seeing much in the way of other options. Daniel had promised to send me a couple of referrals, but his number one choice got married and moved to Florida with her new wife. His second choice wasn't looking for a new job at the moment, which left me in a space that looked quite a bit like Square One.

Daniel agreed there could be benefits to asking Curtis, but suggested I spend a little more time sifting through applications before making him an offer. We both assumed Curtis would never agree to interview for his old job, so if I wanted to hire him, I needed to be one hundred percent sure before bringing it up. Meanwhile, Linda helped me prepare for the upcoming hearings on my schedule as much as she could.

My background in law made reviewing the documents easy, and Jason served as a great sounding board when I had questions. We saw eye-to-eye on most major issues, even if we didn't always have the same reasons. But he had his own constituents, his own agenda. Issues important to New Yorkers living in the Bronx weren't necessarily the same ones that mattered to the residents of Saratoga Springs. It wasn't as easy as seeing who wrote a bill, checking their party, and voting for or against based on their affiliations. I wanted to hire someone to help me focus on the things important to the people in my district.

When Steve suggested on Friday afternoon that we spend the weekend sightseeing, I was so excited I almost hugged him. To be honest, I'd thought our conversation at lunch had been one of those things where people are randomly talking about how it might be nice to do something together at some unspecified future time. Knowing he'd meant the offer made me smile.

After spending most of the week floundering to keep afloat, it would be nice to kick back and have some fun. I hadn't seen or talked to him much over the past few days since his job took him all over the state and I was busy at work. The thought of spending time with him outside of the office appealed to me.

He picked me up at eight-thirty on Saturday morning, and we were on our way. I insisted we take my car so as not to give away any surprises about our destination. Also, I hated playing navigator. When I'm the only one who knows where we're going, let me get us there. The last guy I dated never let me drive, and it always caused arguments, so I was pleasantly surprised when Steve put his keys away and walked to my passenger door without a word. Score one for the lobbyist.

We stopped for takeout coffee at a locally owned shop on the main drag, then headed toward the highway. Steve sat quietly, watching out the windows and occasionally hazarding a guess about our destination. For my part, I kept my eyes on the road and refused to answer any questions other than about my music preferences.

It wasn't long before I turned into the entrance for Saratoga Spa State Park. It was a beautiful place, well worth exploring, but the park itself was not our ultimate destination. I followed the signs for one of the mineral springs located inside the park. Ten minutes later, I pulled into a parking lot and found a space.

After we got out of the car, I held one hand out to Steve. "Right this way."

Together we approached a small gazebo sitting beside the path. The cover measured only a few feet by a few feet, just enough to protect the stone structure inside from the elements.

Steve stopped when he read the sign. "Hold up. You brought me to see water? That's the famous Capital District sight where you take all the tourists? Because, contrary to what you may have heard on TV, we do have water in the City."

"It's not like I'm going to turn on a tap and watch it swirl down the drain," I explained patiently. "This is Karista Spring. Saratoga has twenty-one public fountains, or mineral springs, each with its own distinctive flavor."

"Water has flavor?"

"After today, you will never ask that question again, my friend," I said. "Each spring also has specific health benefits. For example, local residents once thought the mud around this spring helped with arthritis."

"Okay, now I know you're messing with me."

"Believe what you will." The power of the mind was strong, and even if the springs only had a placebo effect, who was to say they didn't bring people comfort? Not having arthritis, I couldn't comment. But Nonna used to love visiting the springs.

From there, we moved over to Geyser Trail, which covered nearly three miles and passed three other springs. The weather was perfect for a long walk through the park, and after being cooped up in the office all week, having an excuse to stretch my legs felt amazing.

"You know, all joking aside," Steve said after we left our third stop, "this is a great way to spend the day. Walking in the sun with a smart, sexy woman. Learning about the area. And oddly, I think this may even help me get votes for the Schools Zoning and Protection Act."

"Oh, yeah?" Part of me wanted to squeal because he'd called me sexy, but this wasn't the time. I could gush like a schoolgirl on Facetime with Mel later. "Does the bill talk about historic or educational sites?"

He shook his head. "No, but it talks about what goes where. I know people think zoning is dull, and it does, but those laws protect our society. You wouldn't want, for example, someone to put a meatpacking plant right next to the historic springs, filling the air with animal noises or polluting the groundwater with their waste. Right?"

"Of course not." Lost in thought for a moment, I wrinkled my nose. "That's not allowed now, is it? I admit, zoning isn't my area, but it seems like big or smelly factories are usually on the outskirts, by themselves."

"It varies by location. All cities and counties have their own zoning regulations. The bill is about closing loopholes that might allow something bad to go in next to something pure and beautiful, like this spring here." He shrugged. "Like I said, it's pretty straightforward. We're getting some pushback because Rumsfeld wastes so much time playing party politics. Some people are likely to vote no on principle."

"Ugh. That's so annoying."

"You're telling me. It's my job to get people to pass laws, and nowhere does my training have a section called 'Dealing With Unreasonable People.'"

"That must be frustrating." I reached over and squeezed his hand.

In response, he smiled at me. "Thanks. I like how you get me."

"I do, but to be fair, I also get the urge to vote no to make Rumsfeld mad. That guy is a piece of work."

"You wouldn't dare!"

"No. The voters deserve better," I said. "They also deserve better than to have him represent them, but one thing at a time. I still have to review the bill again, but at first glance, it's an easy yes."

"It is," he said. "And the vote's not for another week. That's plenty of time! You'll be fine."

We walked along the trail, our hands occasionally brushing as we took in the trees. Saratoga Spa State Park housed some beautiful hiking trails. It was the perfect spot to spend a warmish spring morning getting to know each other. And by the time we stopped at our fourth spring of the day, he agreed it was possible the water tasted a little different at each of them.

Once we left the park, I drove to our next destination.

"High Rock Spring? You really like your water, huh?" Steve asked when I stopped the car.

"Well, yes, but I also like food." I pointed across the street. "And this restaurant has amazing French onion soup."

"Now you're talking!"

"—which we will try after tasting the spring," I said. "Come on. Legend says this one confers health and strength."

He shook his head with a good-natured smile, but followed. By the time we settled into our seats for lunch, he'd shifted to talking about how cool it was to have a town built on so many natural geysers. I carefully avoided saying "I told you so." At least until Steve declared the soup to be "absolutely amazing."

"Remind me to eat here as often as possible," he said. "It's as good as my favorite place in the City."

"Oh, yeah? That's high praise! Should we alert the local papers?"

"Very funny." He hesitated. "Hey, I don't want you to think this is too forward of me, but…"

"But what?"

He shook his head and looked away. "Never mind. It was a dumb idea."

"Don't be embarrassed. You can tell me."

Steve stopped and studied his shoes. "I was looking around, thinking about how different this area is from where I grew up, and then I remembered how you've never been there. Do you want to go home with me?"

"To meet your parents?" I tried to keep the incredulousness out of my voice, but inviting me home was awfully forward. We hadn't even kissed yet.

To my great relief, Steve laughed, a big bellow that echoed through the trees. "No, oh god, no. I mean, they're lovely people. But no."

"Thank goodness."

"Sorry, I'm nervous and that came out all wrong. Let's go into the City tomorrow. Catch the early train, walk around, see the sights. Drink some water. I mean, it won't be fancy like your hot springs, but it'll quench your thirst."

"Don't knock the springs, man." I hesitated. "I want to, really. But I don't know. I've got my first big Senate hearing on Friday, and without a Chief of Staff, there's no one to help me prepare. I know most of what's on the calendar seems like an easy decision, but I need to read all the documents. I'm still a newbie Senator. It's my first floor vote. Although I sincerely doubt anyone cares about my opinion, I want to at least be able to articulate the reasoning behind each of my votes, whether yes or no."

Pleading filled his eyes. "Come on, please? You've got all week to prepare. It won't take you long to go through everything. We can read on the train."

He looked so earnest; I hated to disappoint him. Besides, a day in New York City did sound like fun. I was curious to see the place I'd only visited in books and the movies. The love Steve held for his hometown was apparent. Part of me longed to feel the same connection to a place, any place. Sure, Albany was great, but it didn't make my face light up like when Steve talked about going to visit home. I could use some magic in my life.

"Okay, I'm in." Leaning forward across the table, I gave him a soft kiss on the lips. Our first kiss, and it was every bit as full of promise as I'd hoped. Steve's lips were so soft. He cupped my cheeks and kissed me with such tenderness, I wanted to melt against him.

This wasn't the time or the place, though. Reluctantly, I pulled away. "Now hurry up and finish your soup. We've got more springs to see."

Chapter Eight

Our train arrived in New York City mid-morning the next day. The sun shone brightly, and the temperature was warm, so Steve suggested we walk instead of taking a cab. Having never been to Manhattan, I eagerly agreed. Who wanted to see the sights from inside a taxi on such a gorgeous spring day?

As we moved along the crowded sidewalks, I peppered him with questions about where we were going. He deflected them all. Finally, he grabbed my hand and pulled me to a halt at a crosswalk. "Ta-da! Here we are."

"The Apple Store!" I clasped my hands over my heart and batted my eyes at him. "I've always thought this is way better than the mineral springs! How did you know?"

Steve twisted his lips and gave me an exasperated sigh. "Right. We spent half the morning on a train because the Apple Store in Manhattan is better than the one in Albany."

"To be fair, I don't think there's been a shooting at this one."

"Touché." Leaning forward, he tweaked my nose. "Stop being deliberately obtuse and look at the reason we're here."

"Oh, you mean the massive expanse of trees? It's cute. Almost as pretty as the Adirondacks. You know, the big forest that covers a hundred and sixty miles of land upstate?"

"I like when you play hard to get." His eyes twinkled at me. I liked it, too. It had been years since a man pursued me, and the banter was absolutely half the fun for me. I loved this push and pull, the will-he-or-won't-he. The thrill of his hand in mine. "Anyway, to our left, you will see Central Park, the jewel in the crown of New York City."

"The jewel? That doesn't sound right. Hold on sec." I pulled out my phone and tapped away for a moment. "A-ha! The jewel in the crown of New York City is Old City Hall."

He put his hands on his hips. "Are you going to let me show you around or not? I let you drag me to taste a bunch of water yesterday. Which, I might add, all tasted *like water*."

Ouch.

"Don't let the people of Saratoga Springs hear you say that. Maybe drinking from the East River has dulled your taste buds." But I shot him a dazzling smile and put my phone back in my bag. It felt so good to be outside, flirting with a man I found irresistible. I'd been so busy logging hours at my old law firm, I hadn't let myself cut loose and have fun nearly often enough. I couldn't remember the last time I'd been on a date. "Lead the way, Obi-Wan."

"That's more like it." He tugged at my hand. "You're going to love this."

We started at Strawberry Fields, a monument to the Beatles. They were way before my time, so I didn't care too much for my own sake, but Dad loved them. I'd mentioned it at lunch in a throwaway comment I barely remembered. The fact that Steve brought me here made me smile. What a sweet gesture. I took a few shots, even making Steve capture me in various poses, and texted them over. Dad sent back a beaming selfie, which made me doubly glad for taking the time to look around.

Once I'd finished admiring the architecture in the mosaic, Steve and I headed deeper inside the park, crisscrossing around the paths to the various attractions.

Even though it was still before lunch, the line for Shakespeare in the Park wound around endlessly, so we didn't even talk about going to see a show. Too bad. It would've been fun, but I didn't want to spend my only afternoon in the City standing in line. Even if it was a gorgeous day.

Still, I stood there for a minute, chewing my lower lip, wondering if it was worth looking to see what show we'd be missing.

"Next time," Steve said. "I promise. They have a handful of seats for sale. If we plan ahead, we can get them."

The mention of a "next time" made up for missing out on the show, so I followed him to our next destination. A giant brick structure with music coming from the inside. A gazebo? There were so many people in the park, my five-foot-four-inch self couldn't tell what we were looking at until we drew much closer.

"The carousel!" I clapped my hands together and jumped up and down. "I've always wanted to go on the carousel!"

"That look on your face makes this entire day worth it. I'm so glad we did this."

"Me, too. Thank you so much."

"No, thank you." Steve pulled me close and cupped my chin in his hands. Electricity shot down my spine. I looked up at him, marveling at my good luck. He leaned forward, pressing his lips against mine.

It was gentle, sweet. A perfect kiss in Central Park. The type that made me hope we would have more perfect kisses in our future, preferably sooner rather than later.

Once we got to the front of the line, I walked up and down

between the horses, taking my time before making a decision. I patted a red saddle here, a brown mane there. At one point, I paused beside a bench, thinking. The bench would seat both of us, letting me snuggle close to Steve. Snuggling could lead to more kissing, and I liked kissing him. However, it only went round and round—it wasn't on one of the pulleys that lifted the horses. The bench wouldn't give me the full experience.

Finally, I settled on a black horse with gold decorations and a blue saddle. "This one. Black Beauty was my favorite book as a kid."

"Black Beauty it is," Steve said. "Do you need help getting up?"

In response, I shot him a withering look. Chivalry was great and all, but I could climb a ten-foot pole using only my forearms. I didn't need help mounting a fake horse.

"Right. Sorry. You are fully capable."

"And don't you forget it." Quickly, I swung onto my chosen steed. Steve took the mount on the outside, which was a gorgeous shade of teal. I gestured. "What's yours named?"

"Green Beauty, natch."

"How original," I said. "Also, your horse is teal."

Before he could answer, the organ music picked up volume, and a voice came over the loudspeaker. We were off! The horses moved up and down, traveling around the room side by side. On the sidelines, unfamiliar faces blurred together. Everyone looked so happy, carefree. Beside me, Steve looked as full of wonder as a child. There was something magical about this experience. Despite all my barbs and my staunch defense of the Capital District, I understood why Steve loved New York City so much. Big cities each had their own energy, and the energy here was joyfully infectious.

When he caught my eye, he threw his arms out to the side, leaned forward, and beamed at me. "I'm the king of the world!"

A loud peal of laughter escaped me. From the moment I'd arrived for my first day of work at the Senate, I'd been a ball of stress and frustration. No more. All the negative emotions streamed down my back like water off a duck. I felt amazing. Throwing my head back, I raised my arms and basked in the air rushing across my body as we picked up speed.

The next time I glanced to my right, Steve did the same, moving down as my horse went up and vice versa. Ahead, the churning poles mesmerized me. Watching the U-shaped hook move, leading the horses up, then down, made me feel oddly at peace. Kind of like meditating, but faster.

Steve's voice interrupted my thoughts. "Tell me something. Can you climb to the top?"

Before answering, I studied the metal rod connecting my horse to the structure. It was a few inches wide, about the same circumference as some of the thicker poles I'd used for competition. Early in my training, I'd learned poles with a bigger diameter tended to work better for me for climbing. Going up this one would be simple. Show-offy, but simple.

I glanced around. I wasn't supposed to. Sure, it was Steve's idea, but I was my own person. I'd done a lot to ignore the stripper rumors, making a point never to address them head-on. I responded with lawyer jokes, or innuendo, or with redirecting, or by simply walking away. Climbing up a pole in public wouldn't say "not a stripper." Then again—that was everyone else's problem, not mine. Steve and I were here to have fun. Hanging from the top of the carousel sounded like fun. Besides, it was a once-in-a-lifetime thing. When would I be back here?

Decision made. I raised one finger to my lips. "Shh."

He made the "zipped lips" gesture, and we shared a conspiratorial smile. With another glance over my shoulder, I reached high above my head and grabbed the pole over the horse's head. Slipping my feet from the fake stirrups, I pulled.

My body rose, and I reached my legs up, pointing my toes into a perfect vee shape. I didn't press my luck by climbing all the way to the top.

Especially because this pole moved up and down, while the ones I used for training spun in a circle. The last thing I needed was to go flying off the carousel. I'd probably flatten a small child.

"Wow," Steve breathed. "That's amazing."

"Hey! You there! No funny business!"

Oops. Caught in the act. Quickly, I settled back into my seat and threw out an apology. Steve pressed his lips together, shoulders shaking in silent laughter.

"Don't let me see that again!" The man in the booth yelled.

As soon as our horses moved out of sight, we dissolved into giggles.

"Well, color me impressed," Steve said when we regained control of ourselves.

"Thanks. A lot of pole stuff looks fancy, but it's not tricky. Just requires dedication and persistence."

"Like most things in life that are worth the effort."

Our eyes met, and I flashed back to our kiss. Yes, many things in life were worth investing time and patience. Like starting a new relationship.

Then we circled back by the operator, who glared at us. The two of us dissolved into laughter a second time.

By the time the ride ended, our bond was cemented. We were like teenagers let loose for the first time on their own. We continued exploring, circling by the duck pond and flying high on the swings before we meandered back toward the Metropolitan Museum of Art. Steve called it "The Met," but I didn't feel like the museum and I were on a first-name basis yet. All I knew about it came from a book I'd read in the third grade about two kids who ran away and lived there.

I took everything in with wide eyes and a feeling of pure joy.

"So what's next?" I asked.

"Nope. Not telling. You'll have to wait."

"Come on, please?" I batted my lashes.

"Do you have a bug in your eye?" Steve asked innocently.

Humph. So much for my feminine wiles. "Just give me one little hint."

"Fine. Patience and Fortitude."

"You're telling me if I have patience and fortitude, you'll tell me where we're going? That's not helpful. That's like saying 'good things come to those who wait.'"

"That is also true." He spent a moment taking in my blank stare before smirking at me. "What? You wanted a hint. You've got one. Patience and Fortitude. That's your hint."

Whatever. Two could play this game. Whipping my phone out, I pulled up my web browser and typed in exactly what he said. Before the results could finish loading, the phone vanished from my hand.

"Hey!"

"You're cheating!"

"It's not cheating to utilize your resources effectively."

"Spoken like a true politician." He put my phone in the front pocket of his hoodie. "I'm keeping this. You can have it back at the end of the day."

Inwardly, I seethed. I mean, sure, I shouldn't be googling on our date, but that was *my* phone. I let out a huff but pretended to give up. There wasn't a need for my phone right now, anyway. Steve knew his way around the City, and if we somehow got separated, well, some wise soul had laid Manhattan out in a grid. I could get back to the train station without too much trouble. Or, you know, hail a cab. That wasn't the point.

Maybe there was a way I could get it back and make this afternoon a little more interesting.

Leaning in, I wrapped my arms around his waist, pulling him close. He grinned down at me. For a moment, I reveled in the feel of his lean, muscled back beneath my hands, but this was no time to get distracted.

"Mmm," Steve said. "This is nice."

"Thank you for bringing me to see your hometown. I'm having a great day."

"Me, too." He bent down, capturing my lips with his.

The kiss was soft, gentle, just like him, but something brewed beneath the surface. A passion I wanted very badly to explore. My left hand rubbed his back while my right moved forward, running along his flat abs. Reaching inside, I found the thing I sought and pulled it out.

"Got it!" Waving my phone over my head, I danced a little jig of victory as I spun away, out of reach.

Steve watched me, his face a mixture of expressions I couldn't quite make out. Then he lunged for me.

I jumped back, out of his reach.

"Lana, no!"

The laughter on my face turned into a shriek as I fell backward. My arms spun, I teetered on my heels, and then I fell into the pond.

Water cascaded across my vision. My butt hit the bottom of the pond. I sputtered for a moment beneath the surface before realizing the water was so shallow here, I could sit up. Seconds later, my face broke the surface. Despite the cool water, my cheeks flamed with humiliation.

Oh, man. We were having such a perfect day and then…. I looked up into his laughing eyes, and suddenly it didn't matter. It was still a wonderful day. The sun was shining; I had a fun and interesting guy by my side. So I'd gotten a little wet? Wasn't the first time my clumsiness caused a bit of embarrassment, wouldn't be the last. It was a reasonably warm day, my clothes would dry, and if they didn't, we were in the shopping capital of the state.

Steve reached down to help me up. I took his hand gratefully, then tugged sharply. His laughter turned to an "O" of surprise. He landed with a splash beside me.

The wave of water washing across my face only made me laugh harder. By the time we regained control of ourselves, people were starting to stare, but I didn't care.

"Aren't dancers supposed to be graceful?" Steve asked once we finally got ourselves on firm ground.

"Bite me." At my words, Steve leaned forward, a glint in his eyes as if preparing to do just that. Then I realized I still clutched my now-dripping phone in my left hand. A groan escaped me.

"Oh, no. What did I do?"

He shrugged. "It's okay. It's waterproof. Turn it off and let it dry, but it should be fine. Just, you know, you can't Google anything for a few hours."

"Don't joke about that." I shuddered. "I might not make it."

"It's OK. I'll take care of you," he said.

While the sun dried us off, we explored Fifth Avenue, moving in and out of stores I'd never be able to afford to shop at. I did jot down some ideas and take pictures for dresses to make myself when I had time. Not to mention somewhere to wear a full-length opera gown with gloves. Then Steve steered me to the New York City Public Library, which turned out to be guarded by two lions.

"Here we are!" He grinned broadly and gestured. "Lana, I'd like you to meet Patience and Fortitude."

"The lions?"

"That's right."

"The lions guarding the library have names?"

"Yes. Just like characters in a story."

"Hmmph." After a moment, I begrudgingly admitted his hint sucked less than I'd originally thought.

The library was absolutely stunning. The architecture took my breath away, and to be honest, I'd never thought of myself as someone to care about that stuff. But beauty is beauty, in whatever form you find it. Besides, sometimes architecture inspired fashion, and I loved pretty clothes.

As if he heard my thoughts, Steve led me around the corner and down a hallway. At first, I wondered if he was dragging me off to further explore our kiss in the park. But then he pushed open a door to a room housing an exhibit. I gasped and spun around. "Fashion! You brought me to a fashion exhibit!"

My voice echoed off the ceiling, and people spun to look. Oops. "Sorry! I love clothes."

A woman near the door smiled at me, then gave me a pamphlet. "It's okay, dear. Enjoy."

Turning to Steve, I said, "How did you know?"

"That you love fashion?" He grinned at me. "I may have bribed your secretary with a sandwich from the place that only sells grilled cheese."

"Hold on." My hands went to my hips, but I deliberately kept my voice to a whisper. "You went to the grilled cheese place *without me?*"

"A mistake I plan to correct at the first possible opportunity." He kissed the tip of my nose. "You're cute when you're pissed."

"Flattery will get you almost as far as sandwiches," I grabbed his hand. "Let's go look around. Hey, that reminds me. What do lawyers wear to court?"

He glanced around as if the answer might be found on one of the mannequins lining the walls.

"Lawsuits!"

Steve groaned. "You just got less cute."

"Liar."

We moved deeper into the exhibit. After I geeked out for a bit at all the clothes, we wandered the street with giant ice cream cones, chatting about everything and nothing. I told Steve all about moving around so much as a kid, about meeting Mel in high school when we were both in Germany, about how I came to be a Senator, never mentioning the stripper rumors. I did tell him I'd litigated worker's compensation claims, so he could draw his own conclusions.

Steve talked about growing up in the City. His parents still lived in the house he grew up in, a concept completely foreign to me. He told me about living at home while going to college, about getting into politics, and what it was like to travel all over the state for business. We didn't have much in common, but it didn't matter. I enjoyed his company.

Finally, it was time to head over to 42nd Street to catch dinner and a show. I'd been to many plays in many cities over the years, but this was my first time on Broadway. I sat on the edge of my seat throughout the entire show, eyes wide with wonder. By the time we took the subway back to Penn Station for the train back to Albany, we collapsed onto our seats, happily exhausted.

By the time the train pulled into the station, it was after midnight. The thought of asking Steve to come home with me crossed my mind, but I had to get up early, and I was practically falling asleep. With so much on the calendar this week, I didn't want to feel like I was shirking my obligations already.

"Thank you so much for a wonderful day," I said as we walked to our cars.

"You know, it doesn't have to end."

"I wish that were true, but I have a long day tomorrow."

He pretended to pout, then broke into a devastating smile.

"I get it. Thanks for coming with me today. I had a great time."

"Me, too."

"And now you agree New York City is the greatest place in the world?"

I pretended to consider it. "I'm not sure. After all, you didn't show me any drinkable water."

He laughed, and we continued the walk in silence, our fingers intertwined.

At the kiss Steve gave me when we got to my Honda, my knees buckled. I almost changed my mind about not inviting him home. Who needed sleep? But I had a long history of falling into things, and I was determined to take my time here. Let our relationship develop naturally.

With regret, I finally pulled away. "I'll see you at work tomorrow?"

"Unfortunately, no. I have to head to Buffalo for a few days. Talk to a few local officials about some proposed school board regulations."

"Sounds riveting."

"Oh, you have no idea," he said. "I'll be back Thursday afternoon. Have dinner with me?"

"I can't wait."

Chapter Nine

The next morning, Jason surprised me at my office door with coffee. "Good morning! Everything okay?"

"Better now. You're my new best friend." By the time I got home from the train station, it was late. My busy weekend had taken a lot out of me, I wouldn't trade it for anything. Jason grinned as I gratefully took my first sip and let out a sigh of pleasure. Perfect. Hot, strong, and black, exactly the way I liked it. "To what do I owe this pleasure?"

"You never replied to my texts yesterday. I was worried."

"Oh! Sorry about that!" One hand smacked my forehead. "I dropped my phone in the pond. It's water-resistant, but I left it off until everything dried out. That reminds me…it's still off. I hope I didn't miss anything else."

"The pond?"

"Yeah, in Central Park. I spent yesterday in the City. My first sight-seeing trip."

"You'd never been?" I shook my head. "You should've told me. I go home on the weekends whenever possible. I would've shown you around."

A slight flush tinged my cheeks. I'd forgotten Jason represented the Bronx. "Thanks, but I was on a date."

"Oh, right." Jason cleared his throat. "Well, glad to hear you're not sick or anything. Your first full session is later this week. I have to head to a meeting, but let me know if you want to go over anything."

"You're the best, thanks," I said. "I've got another Racing, Gaming, and Wagers Commission meeting tomorrow, so that's my first priority."

"You've got this."

The thought of my first full session terrified me and thrilled me in equal parts. But before I got there, I had a billion things to do: reviewing all the bills, reminding myself who everyone was so I didn't embarrass myself, hiring a Chief of Staff... I needed to get on that. Even a temp would be better than nothing. And with that thought, I picked up my phone.

Curtis adamantly refused to even pitch in temporarily. "It's nothing personal, but for the first time in my life, I can take as much time off as I want, and I'm going to. We booked a three-week cruise to Hawaii."

"Lucky. Can I come?"

"You wish," he said. "Have I ever thanked you for taking my job and giving me all this free time?"

"We're becoming friends. Don't make me hate you."

"Listen, call me if you have any questions about stuff. I'm here for you. Just not in the sense of actually showing up at the office."

After we finished chatting, I went back to my flood of applications. Linda happily took over the job of checking everyone's social media before forwarding their resumé to me, which took a lot of the load off, but added a step we didn't have time for. Until we found someone, it was the two of us—and I didn't fully know how to do my job yet.

Jason helped as much as he could, and I appreciated it, but

he had a busy schedule of committee hearings on top of everything else, and someone had staged a primary challenge to his seat, so he was busy campaigning already. Since no one was running against me until possibly November, at least one thing was off my plate at the moment. Three elections in one year were at least two too many.

Hey Siri, set reminder: ask Daniel whether I have an opponent for November.

At some point, I also needed a communications director, but ideally, the Chief of Staff would help with hiring one. After all, I needed people who worked well together. Too bad Daniel couldn't take the job. At the rate I was going, my term would end before we filled any of my open positions. The thought of having to add time for campaigning to my schedule when I had no staff to help out with the day-to-day Senate stuff made me hyperventilate.

The job itself, when I got to do it, still excited me. I loved reading over proposed legislation and actually found myself getting giddy when I found a mistake in a bill coming up for a vote. That was absolutely a highlight. Just think, without my interference, landlords might have been able to evict *victims* of domestic violence instead of the *perpetrators.*

Making a difference made me happy. When my date finally rolled around on Thursday afternoon, that made me even happier.

Steve stayed at a hotel when he was in town since he kept his home in the City. Personally, I couldn't imagine why he'd rather pay three times more to live in a place half the size when he was home an average of one night a week, but it was none of my business. What mattered was that we were here and we about to share a lovely dinner. As long as he worked in Albany regularly, I didn't have to wonder how I felt about having a long-distance relationship. He was here most of the time, anyway.

Shortly before the workday ended, I changed into a knee-length emerald green dress with a full skirt. I'd made it myself, so it fit perfectly. The green enhanced the light brown of my eyes, and the neckline fell at just the right place to give a hint of cleavage without letting Steve see too much, too soon. A quick brush of my hair, the addition of a white cardigan, and an application of bright red lipstick completed the look.

As I walked back to my office, my knees shook with excitement. What if I'd over-thought things and this wasn't a date? What if he'd changed his mind about me since last weekend? What if he'd thought about it and decided he wasn't into me? What if he was mad I asked to move the location and wanted to tell me in person? What if…what if…what if?

To my surprise, Steve waited beside Linda's desk when I returned to my office to check my messages one last time before heading out. Our eyes met, and all those thoughts fled. The wide smile on Steve's face made me blush. He'd left his suit jacket and tie behind, opting instead for a navy cashmere sweater and gray pants. At work, Steve wore his hair neatly parted and combed flat, but tonight he'd used gel to spike it up a bit in the front. Date attire, absolutely. He looked delicious.

"This is a pleasant surprise," I said. "I thought we were meeting at the restaurant."

"I didn't want to wait to see you."

"Where's Linda?"

"Oh, I'm such a dope," he said. "I decided to surprise her with an iced coffee, but forgot the straw. She insisted I wait for you while she went to the cafeteria to grab one."

"That was sweet of you."

"Yeah, well, I only get half credit." He held out one hand. "Shall we?"

"Just a minute. I need to finish a few things before we go." I checked my watch. "I'd apologize, but you're still ten minutes early. Have a seat."

"Actually, in that case, I'll pop out for a minute. I need to talk to Gretchen about next week's schedule."

In my inbox, I found a stack of papers Linda had left for me. Most of this was from earlier in the day when I'd been sitting in on a Ways and Means Committee hearing. Nothing urgent. Then I made one last sweep of the office: voicemail notifications dark, no unread email that couldn't wait, cute guy waiting to take me to dinner.

Linda held up her coffee when I passed through the office. "You've got a keeper there."

"Thanks." I beamed at her. "I hope you're right. You got any exciting plans tonight?"

She shook her head. "Just my daughter Grace. She's been having some issues with her husband, so I want to call for a real heart-to-heart."

"Everything okay?"

"Between you and me, she'd be better off without the guy." Linda sighed. "But she loves him, so for her sake, I hope I'm wrong. Have a good night."

"You, too!"

Steve met me in the hallway outside the door and held out one hand. "Ready?"

"Absolutely."

"By the way, you look stunning." As soon as we exited the building, he leaned over and kissed me softly. Any of my earlier doubts still lingering fled at the contact. The heat was still there, simmering beneath the surface.

"Thanks." I took his hand for the short walk to the restaurant. "You don't look so bad yourself. How was Buffalo?"

"Oh, the usual," he said. "Ridiculous amounts of snow, especially for April. Lots of wind. Colder than Rumsfeld's black heart."

I let out such a loud peal of laughter, people turned to look.

Any remaining nerves evaporated. We chatted easily the rest of the way to the restaurant.

The place I'd chosen wasn't terribly ritzy, but I'd heard good things about the food. Immediately when we entered, the atmosphere made me feel comfortable. At one end, chefs cooked in the open kitchen, letting everyone get a bit of a show. High ceilings with wooden beams and chandeliers gave the interior a rustic look. A cabinet over the bar showcased an impressive array of alcohol, but I wouldn't be drinking tonight. As much as I was looking forward to this dinner, I couldn't afford to linger or to get drunk. I needed to get home and finish working before I turned into a pumpkin.

Our food arrived quickly, and every bite was delicious. Even better than I'd been told to expect. While we ate, I gave Steve the gossip from the Capital—being careful not to share anything that wasn't public knowledge—and he told me all about his wild goose chase trip to Buffalo. He refused to go into the details, but said his chances of success on this one felt about as good as the odds of selling a refrigerator to a polar bear.

Before I knew it, our waiter arrived to ask if we'd like to see a dessert menu.

"Oh, I shouldn't," I said. Too much sugar on a full-stomach would make me sleepy. Even if the description on the menu made my mouth water.

"Come on," Steve said. "You've got to have the fried ice cream. It's amazing."

"I've never understood fried ice cream. Doesn't it melt?" Cooking was not my forte. When I was in college and law school, Mel made most of my meals. She loved cooking, I loved making clothes, it was a match made in heaven. We took the money we saved on eating out or shopping and splurged on pole fitness classes until Mel became an instructor. After I graduated, we each decided to live alone for a change, and I'd intentionally bought a condo near an excellent selection of takeout restaurants. My kitchen was more likely to need a good dusting than to be scoured. Needless to say, I'd never tried to deep fry anything, much less frozen foods.

"There's only one way to answer your question." His eyes pleaded with me not to end the night so soon. "Look, you can get it with hot fudge and coconut or bananas foster."

Oh, man. My resolve crumbled with every word out of his mouth. That sounded amazing. Not to mention, I was enjoying Steve's company. I didn't want to go home to a cold, empty unit and read by myself when I could stay in this safe, cozy room with a man who fascinated me. I'd been working my butt off all week. I was prepared for tomorrow's vote. Better to stay here and relax than to go home and stress about it all night.

"I'll have one cup of coffee," I said. "With the fried ice cream. Then I have to go home."

"Sounds good. I know you're busy." He gestured to the waitress and relayed our order. "Thanks for making the time to come out with me. I missed you."

One cup of coffee turned into a few. When I finally dragged myself away from the table to relieve my bursting bladder, the sight of the clock on the far wall stopped me dead in my tracks. Somehow we'd been chatting for more than three hours. By far the longest dinner date I'd ever had. But also—it was way too late. I should've been home at least an hour ago.

After a record-fast visit to the ladies' room, I returned to our table and apologized to Steve. "We completely lost track of time. I have to get home to finish preparing for tomorrow."

"No problem." He picked up the check, which I hadn't noticed on the edge of our table, and slipped a credit card inside the black folder.

"Please, let me."

"Don't be ridiculous," he said. "This is a business dinner. My company will pay for it."

I glanced down at my dress, then flashed back to the look

in my eyes when he first saw me in it. "This is a business dinner?"

"Sure. What do you think of paying minimum wage to inmates for the work they do creating products sold by the state for a profit?"

"I think that's a wonderful idea. To be honest, that's something I wanted to bring up—"

He held up one hand. "Enough shop talk. But now, this is officially a business dinner."

For a moment I felt affronted that he didn't want to hear my opinion, but then I realized what he was doing. "Next time, if you want a write-off, we need to talk business. I don't like taking advantage of your company. To be honest, I'd feel better if you let me pay."

"Relax, I'm joking," he said. "I get a per diem, and I missed lunch today because I was driving back. It's fine."

"Okay, thanks. Not that I don't love shop talk. I'm saying, we should either save it for the office or make it an official business meeting."

"Agreed. I could listen to you talk politics all day and night," he said. "But not now, because I've got to get you home."

Our server returned, and Steve signed the check before getting my coat for me. Before he closed the cover, I snuck a peek at the total. Back in college, I'd gone on a date with one of the cheapest men alive. He had money but didn't believe in tipping. I'd had to hand cash to our server on the way out. No need tonight. Steve had tipped over thirty percent. I felt mildly relieved. After all, I didn't want to have to dump him before finding out if what we had was as special as I thought it might be.

When he returned with my coat, he held it while I slipped it on, earning more bonus points. Some women hated chivalry, but I loved being treated with respect. Too many people in this world didn't have any respect for anyone; I certainly wasn't going to object to someone being nice to me.

We walked to the parking lot, each lost in our own thoughts, before coming to a halt at my car.

"Thank you for a lovely evening." I smiled up at him. He had the most mesmerizing green flecks in his eyes. And that smile. Oh, his smile was going to get me into trouble.

He leaned forward and placed a soft kiss on my lips. Then he pulled me toward him, swaying ever so slightly against me. I almost groaned at the contact. It had been a long time since I'd dated anyone, and the chemistry between us was electric. Almost like a reflex, my body fitted itself against his.

"Mmmm," I said. "You taste like fried ice cream."

"The night doesn't have to end, you know. Come home with me."

Tempting. Very tempting. After we'd parted on Sunday night, I tossed and turned for an hour thinking about what might have been. But I'd promised myself I wouldn't rush into this, would slow down and enjoy the getting-to-know-you phase of our relationship. After all, we had plenty of time. There was no hurry.

Regretfully, I took a step back. "I can't. I've got a packed day tomorrow, and I need to be well-rested. Lots of hearings and documents to read."

"Pfft. Bill documents are boring. What are you working on? I'll tell you what you need to know in the car. Then you can sleep in tomorrow."

"Thanks, but I prefer to read everything over myself. Must be the lawyer in me. You get it."

His disappointment was so palpable, I wanted to kiss it away. But this wasn't the time. Instead, I pressed my lips against his cheek, near the corner of his mouth. "There will be plenty of time for us later. Don't be disappointed."

He gave me a ghost of a smile. "How could I be disappointed with a promise like that?"

I turned to go. "I'll see you tomorrow, Steve."

"Sweet dreams, Lana. I can't wait for tomorrow."

As I drove home, I thought of his lips against mine, the feel of his body. Sweet dreams, indeed.

Chapter Ten

Over the years, I'd seen the legislative chamber on television enough times that walking across the red carpet and passing by the pillars felt surreal. The gold brick on the walls somehow seemed cozy rather than imposing, which I never would have guessed. Then again, the high ceilings created an echo, giving every word an air of importance. Looking up at the balcony seats, remembering how I'd come to watch legislative sessions in law school, left me marveling at how far I'd come in a few short years. I felt like the luckiest woman in the world.

I, Lana Chen, was a sitting state senator, about to take part in votes to improve the life of New York residents. Not only the people of Saratoga, but statewide. The weight of history in the building brought tears to my eyes.

As the Majority Leader went through the roll call, I glanced down at the printed agenda I'd barely managed to yank from Linda's hand as I screeched by my office after getting stuck in traffic on my way in this morning.

To my surprise, I spotted an extra item on the agenda that hadn't been there before: The first vote was for the Schools

Zoning and Protection Act. That couldn't be right. The SZPA wasn't scheduled until next week. I hadn't had time to review the full text yet!

My heart pounded. How had this happened?

Taking a deep breath, I forced myself to think. Pulling my calendar out, I flipped through it. Okay, I hadn't completely lost my mind. The SZPA was down for next week. It must've been moved at the last minute. How annoying. They couldn't be bothered to notify me?

At least I'd skimmed the bill a couple of days ago. I'd planned to re-read the amendments over the weekend so I'd be prepared for Monday's session, but everything I remembered had seemed like no big deal. Like Steve had told me, the bill strengthened existing zoning provisions by making it more clear where certain types of businesses could be opened. From what I knew, it should be an easy decision.

"Senator Chen?"

With a start, I realized everyone was looking at me. Roll call had ended, and the vote had begun. The Senate Majority Leader went by district number, and they'd somehow made it all the way to the forties without me realizing. Leaning forward, I spoke firmly, hoping to project the certainty in my voice. "Aye."

My first Senate vote. I should've asked Jason to take a picture for my parents. Or Steve could've done it from the balcony. Mom and Dad would be so proud. Oh, well. There were plenty of official photos of the legislature out there. Or maybe they could watch me on public access next week.

As my thoughts wandered along these lines, my gaze fell on Jason. In response to my smile, he pressed his lips together and averted his eyes. Weird. As far as I knew, nothing needed to be said other than "aye" or "nay," but it looked like I'd somehow made a mistake. Did the microphone not amplify my voice well enough? I should check the volume.

A few seats to my left, a Republican Senator also voted "aye." Weird. I'd expected this one to be split along party lines. Then a Democratic Senator from Buffalo voted no. Senator Wolf voted yes, which surprised me. He was one of the more conservative members of the Racing, Gaming, and Wagers Commission. Something was off.

Time slowed. I looked around the room, trying to make eye contact with anyone, but half the floor didn't know who I was and the rest were busy with the vote. My growing sense of unease grew stronger when Majority Leader Diaz voted nay. Not that I believed in always voting along party lines—thinking for myself and making my own decisions were more important than blind loyalty—but between the vote discrepancies and Jason's refusal to meet my eyes, I definitely missed something.

Suddenly, I didn't think the problem was with my microphone.

After the senator from District 63 cast the final vote, Minority Leader Rumsfeld leaned forward. "That's thirty-two aye votes, thirty-one nays. The ayes have it. Motion passed."

The rest of the morning was a blur of hearings and speeches. I took careful notes, determined not to get caught unprepared again. I'd been lucky my first vote wasn't anything major, although I didn't get why the vote came out the way it did. Politics as usual, I guessed. How sad. If I stayed in this seat —and I was pretty sure I wanted to—I'd make a point of reaching across the aisle when I could. We had to put the people of New York ahead of party loyalty. Sure, my party had the majority now, but that could change. I wanted to encourage people to think for themselves and to do the right thing, no matter whose name was on a piece of legislation.

Most of the remaining items on the agenda were fairly mundane: a resolution to honor a Rochester man who died saving orphans from a burning building (passed by a landslide); a partisan motion to raise taxes on the middle class (failed by one vote); a bill expanding when cities could apply for state aid (passed by a wide margin); another that clarified the wording of two of the child custody statutes (ditto). Last up was the racing bill that landed me on the Racing, Gaming, and Wagering Committee. With my suggested changes, I was ecstatic to see the bill pass by a landslide, in time for new regulations to take effect when the track opened this summer.

After the final vote, the Majority Leader assigned a stack of new bills to various committees, which reminded me I needed to see what other openings remained. As a long-time party leader, Senator Baker had sat on several, including the much-coveted Appropriations. I wasn't quite ready for that—and his spot wasn't still available—but I didn't have to stick with just Racing, Gaming, and Wagering. Plenty of senators served on multiple committees. I wanted to find something interesting to me, like Labor or Children and Families. I'd love to have a say on more legislation before it got to the final vote, to affect amendments, or even help stop bad bills from getting to the full floor.

When the Senate broke for lunch, I felt confident I'd put in a good morning's work. Jason waited for me outside the door, his expression inscrutable.

"Hey," I said. "I've got plans for lunch. Can we talk later?"

"No. We need to talk now." His voice was so low, I barely heard him. He grabbed my arm, gentle but also firm enough that I knew not to try to shake him off. "Let's go to my office."

"Sure. What's wrong?"

My question remained unanswered. He didn't speak again while we navigated through the crowd. When anyone sought to speak to him, Jason simply nodded and kept moving. He didn't drop my arm until we got to his inner office and the door shut behind us.

"What the hell happened in there?"

I blinked at him. "What are you talking about? My racing bill?"

"No, not the racing bill. The racing bill was good work. I'm talking about the SZPA."

It took me a moment to shift from Jason praising my success to the second half of his statement. But even once I realized what he was saying, I didn't understand the issue. "I voted in favor of urban renewal and development. That's a good thing."

"You're kidding, right? You think the Schools Zoning and Protection Act is going to benefit people? I thought you were a Democrat."

"No, I'm not kidding. It's about expanding opportunities and economic growth."

"It's about…!" He stopped. The way he sputtered, I wanted to undo his tie to make sure he didn't pass out from lack of oxygen. "Did you read the bill? The full text?"

Jason's condescending attitude made me want to yell back that of course I had, what kind of idiot did he think I was? At the same time, he was angry. Way too angry. Something didn't add up. Especially because I never finished reading the amendments. I couldn't defend my vote if I didn't know what part of the text got Jason so upset. Suddenly, I suspected I'd missed something crucial.

"Yes, I read the text! I skimmed over everything, and I was planning to read the amendments this weekend."

"You skimmed part of it. That's what you're saying?"

His words made me even more defensive, not least of all because part of me knew where he was going, and he was right. But I held my ground. "I didn't know the bill was on today's agenda! Why didn't anyone tell me the vote got moved?"

"I don't know." He ran one hand through his hair. "You

should have gotten a call yesterday afternoon. Any chance your assistant forgot to give you the message?"

I glared at him, not even wanting to dignify his insult with a response. "Linda's been with me for years. She doesn't forget to give me messages. Anyway, what gives? From what I read, the bill seemed like an obvious yes. Who doesn't want to protect kids?"

Jason let out a deep sigh and leaned back against his desk. "I thought you were smarter than that."

Finally, my temper flared. "And I thought you were my friend."

"I am your friend, but Lana—you can't vote for a proposal if you didn't read the full text with all the amendments. The things we do here matter. There are consequences for every action. Oh, man, this is so messed up."

"Stop tiptoeing around, Jason. What's going on?"

"The summaries you get for each bill are written by the people who want it to pass. In this case, Rumsfeld's cohorts. You know that."

"Sure, but they're still factual, aren't they?"

"They don't cover every single thing included in the bill," he said. "Especially not the parts that might get people to vote against it. On Monday, the authors added an additional clause because they thought people would be distracted by the special election and not pay attention."

Uh-oh. A feeling of dread started to grow in the pit of my stomach. "What kind of clause?"

"It says that, as part of urban development and renewal, the city council has a right to shut down or refuse permits for any 'inappropriate' business, or businesses likely to draw 'people of unseemly character.'"

His words punched me in the gut. No. This couldn't be happening. It was the exact law Curtis threatened to pass when he was running for election. The very reason Mel ran against him in the first place—and indirectly, the need to keep this type of bill from being passed was the reason I wound up working here.

Suddenly I understand what Gretchen was doing in my office when I first started. And why she refused to tell me. She'd wanted Curtis to help with the SZPA amendments.

I couldn't believe it. By not doing my homework, I'd voted to put my best friend out of business.

Chapter Eleven

Jason's words punched me in the gut. I couldn't believe I'd screwed up so badly. In my desire to shed the weight of expectations, to do what I wanted for a change instead of what was expected of me, I'd gone too far. In my old job, a screw-up of this magnitude would be legal malpractice—it could have gotten me sued. Or fired. That concept didn't translate to working for the legislature, but knowing I'd helped pass a bill that would ruin lives made me want to vomit.

Why didn't anyone tell me the SZPA vote got moved? I never would have gone out to dinner with Steve if I'd known there was work left to do. Or at least I'd have skipped dessert to read the darn thing. We'd been getting along so well, though, and I was so sure the items on today's agenda were no big deal. The only one that should've caused a stir was one no one expected to pass (and it didn't). A senator from the Hamptons introduced it as a way of paying lip service to his constituents, and everyone knew it.

My hands flew to my mouth. "Oh my god. I screwed everything up."

"Yeah, you did."

A moan escaped me. "Thanks for your support."

"What do you want me to say? If you had taken five minutes to talk to me, this could have been avoided. You could have called, texted, or emailed me any time over the past week. We talk every day, and I always ask if you have questions about anything."

"I've been trying to form my own opinions on things."

"How's that working out?" When I opened my mouth, no words came out, so he continued. "I was here all weekend, reviewing the amendments. Where were you?"

The worlds "on a date" were not going to leave my mouth. I couldn't tell Jason I'd screwed up the most important job I'd ever had because I met a guy who made my heart go pitter-pat. This was so bad. And I knew better. My whole life, I hated those girls who dropped everything the minute they had a boyfriend.

Instead of answering Jason's question, I said, "How was I supposed to know they'd hide something so insidious in a run-of-the-mill zoning and urban renewal bill?"

"Oh, I don't know," he said. "Maybe because that's what people always do. Half the laws that get passed have weird, random provisions in there. Look at the Affordable Health Care Act. President Obama made so many compromises to get Republicans to vote for the thing, it doesn't do nearly enough to help the people who need it."

"Okay, sure, but that's universal health care. It's controversial. We're talking about the Schools Zoning and Protection Act!"

"It's sexist. Which you would have known if you weren't so busy cozying up to the head lobbyist working to pass the damn thing."

My insides bristled at his tone. We got bills all the time. People constantly were sending me documents to read. This is why I needed a Chief of Staff. To summarize, to hit the key passages—and this is also why the Senate had dozens of committees. Committees were supposed to discuss the bills, kill stuff when they could. Proposed legislation should never make it to a full floor vote with secret provisions tucked inside.

And it wouldn't have, if I'd been doing my job.

"This has nothing to do with me and Steve," I insisted.

"This has everything to do with you and Steve," Jason said. "He played you. He lied and charmed you to get you to vote for the bill. Which I would've told you if you weren't so completely infatuated with him that you couldn't see anyone else."

I sighed. "Let's leave Steve out of this. I know you don't like him. You know I do. I don't believe he was using me, and at the moment, it doesn't matter. We need to fix this. How do I get another vote?"

"You can't," he said simply.

Another groan escaped me, this one half a sob.

What an idiot I'd been. After working so hard all these years, I'd ruined everything. Worse, I'd put my best friend out of business. All because I'd somehow not seen a message. It was probably sitting on my desk. I'd been in such a hurry to get to dinner with Steve, I missed it.

A faint glimmer of hope came to me. Like the federal system, New York's legislature had two houses. Both needed to pass a law before it was sent on to the governor for a signature. Since this bill was drafted by a member of the Senate, the next step was for the Assembly to decide whether to pass the law.

Unless I got to them first. "Hold on. When's the Assembly voting?"

"They filed in right after we left," Jason said. "They're voting right now."

I didn't even stop to think. Didn't respond. Instead, I turned and raced out of the office. The speed at which I'd run to make this morning's hearings on time got completely left in the dust. Most of the Senate members had thankfully already returned to their offices, so there weren't too many people to see me running down the halls like someone set my hair on fire.

Moments later, the door came into view. I increased my pace, barely aware of the second set of footsteps echoing on the floor behind me.

"That's it, then." A voice I assumed belonged to the Speaker of the Assembly carried through the door to my ears. Having never met the man, I couldn't be sure. But the Assembly was definitely in session. I yanked the door open.

Inside the room, a short, stout man with curly red hair and thick, square glasses held the room's attention. He glared at me for a moment but kept talking. "And the ayes have it! The Schools Zoning and Protection Act is passed by a vote of one hundred to fifty."

"Wait!" I said weakly.

"Motion carried." The gavel dropped, echoing through the room like shots to my heart.

It wasn't even close. The bill passed by a landslide. Even if I'd made it, I never would have convinced twenty-six total strangers to change their minds at the last minute. My one chance to stop this thing was to vote "no" when my turn came, and I'd screwed it up.

"Excuse me, ma'am. Can I help you?"

The words stuck in my throat. I couldn't move. Couldn't breathe. Jason came to my rescue. He stepped up to my side and gently grasped my elbow. "Excuse me, Mr. Majority Leader. We made a mistake."

Jason led me out of the room, but as soon as the doors shut behind us, I sagged against him. Too late, again. What a day. Tears rolled down my cheeks, soaking into Jason's collar.

If the governor signed—

A thought struck me, and I took a step back, sniffling. "What about Abbot? Can't she veto?"

"I'm sure she *could*," Jason said. "But she's made no secret of her support for this bill."

No secret to anyone but me, apparently. The whole legislature knew the full contents of this bill, but I was the new girl. I didn't know anyone. Despite Jason's negative comments about Steve, we'd never talked about this vote at all. We'd chatted and spent time together, and okay, maybe I'd let myself get a little too wrapped up in the excitement of what could be happening between us. But he'd never tried to talk to me into voting for the bill, and he'd certainly never lied about the contents. The only person I'd specifically talked to was Gretchen, and she made it sound like the bill was boring. Completely mundane. Nothing of interest.

Gretchen, whose boss was the Senate Minority Leader. One of the bill's co-authors.

Oh, no. What had I done?

I grasped at Jason's words like a lifeline. "I'll have to change her mind. Convince her to veto."

"A terrific plan," he said. "How are you going to do that?"

An excellent question. The governor was on vacation this week, away on some kind of annual family retreat where no one took their devices. Sounded like one of the circles of hell to me —how did anyone get through the day without looking stuff up?

"If she's gone, she can't sign the bill, right?"

He shrugged. "I suppose not. Do you plan to catch her the second she returns?"

I could do that. Camp in the hallway outside her office. Or, I could… go find her and talk to her before she even knew the bill was going to arrive on her desk.

A ludicrous plan, yes. But it might work.

"Nope. I'm going to talk to her."

"Really? Did you forget to mention you're telepathic?"

"Very funny," I said. "I have to find her."

"She's camping in the Adirondacks, at her family's secret camping spot, the location of which has not been revealed to the media in at least twenty years. And you're going to… find her?" He snorted. "Okay. Good luck."

"Either help me or don't. I don't have time for this." At Jason's blank stare, I turned and strode toward my office. I couldn't make a plan with him looking at me like that.

Sure, finding the governor sounded like a brilliant plan, but it wasn't realistic. Once I googled "Where is Governor Abbot's secret vacation spot," I was pretty much out of ideas. What was I going to do?

I couldn't just give up. What would I say to Mel? How could I possibly tell my best friend that I'd single-handedly ruined the dreams I'd pushed her into pursuing?

No. I needed to fix this before she heard the news. We'd been friends for more than ten years, and I couldn't stand her thinking I'd betrayed her so some rich property developers could make more money. Once I stopped Governor Abbot from signing the bill, then I'd tell Mel everything.

By the time I made it to my office, my head felt clearer. Thankfully, Linda had gone to lunch, because I couldn't stand it if she tried to talk me out of what I was about to do. It was a terrible plan, but the only plan I had. There was no time to make a better one. This bill would hit Governor Abbot's desk before midnight. She was due back in the office on Monday morning, but she could drop by her office to sign legislation any time she wanted.

Obviously, I wasn't magic like Jason jokingly suggested, and I had no idea where to find the governor. But I knew someone who might. Picking up my phone, I scrolled through my recent calls before tapping on a name.

He answered immediately. "This better be good. I'm neck-deep in mineral hot springs, preparing for the mud bath of a lifetime."

If he were truly irritated to hear from me, he wouldn't have answered. Knowing that, I ignored his preamble and got straight to the point. "Hey, Curtis. Didn't you say your family used to go camping with Abbot's?"

Chapter Twelve

It turned out, while Curtis's family had gone camping with Governor Abbot's every spring, he didn't have the first clue where the campsite was located. As a teenager, he sat in the back of his parents' SUV, watching DVDs or reading a book rather than paying attention to the route. Because that was what teenagers did.

"Can you ask your dad for me?"

"I could," he said, "but I'm afraid we're not currently speaking."

My heart sank. I was desperately aware Jason didn't believe I could make this happen, and the last thing I wanted was to have to give up before I'd even started. There had to be a way to get to her. "Please, Curtis. This is urgent. I need to speak to the governor as soon as possible."

He took a deep breath. "I'm not calling my father. For one thing, he doesn't have a phone right now. But I'll tell you where to find him."

After retiring abruptly from the Senate, Mr. Baker moved into an RV with the family housekeeper. Curtis gave me directions to their most recent campsite, which was thankfully between the legislative offices and the Adirondacks, meaning I wouldn't have to spend half the day driving out of my way to track him down.

My purse was in my hand before I'd finished thanking Curtis. Then I looked down at my outfit. A black skirt suit and four-inch heels were incredibly appropriate for my workday as a Senator. Not so much for traipsing around the woods. I'd have to go home and change. Well, fork.

When I hung up, Steve stood in my doorway waiting patiently for me to finish. "Hey. We still on for lunch?"

Everything Jason had said swirled around in my head. *There is no you and Steve. He played you.* But then I saw the way he was smiling at me, and I couldn't believe it. Sure, I'd only known the guy a couple of weeks. But I couldn't believe he'd spend all this time with me to get me to side with him on one bill. Especially when he couldn't have known I wouldn't get time to read the whole thing.

Miserably, I shook my head. "I screwed up a vote today, and now I have to make things right."

"What are you talking about? Last night, you were all set for today's hearings. Ready to rock it."

"I know, but they moved one of the bills from Monday to today, and I didn't get the message." I sighed. "Of all the terrible luck. I didn't get a chance to finish reading everything, and it turned out there were some bad clauses I didn't know about in one of the bills."

"Oh, Lana, I'm sorry. That happens sometimes."

"Apparently everyone knows that but me." I studied him, trying to figure out what he'd known. Of course he knew what was in the bill if he was working for the people who wanted to pass it, like Jason said. But Steve's face didn't hold a trace of deception.

"It's the kind of thing you'd have heard if they'd done a full orientation for you," he said. "You have a mentor, right? I'm surprised they didn't mention it."

Me, too, actually. Jason's voice in the back of my head warned me that maybe Steve had an ulterior motive, he wanted me to mess up the vote. I squashed it. Why wouldn't Jason have warned me? But his words came back to me—I'd been so busy getting to know Steve, I hadn't taken the time to learn my job properly. The allegation hurt, doubly so because he was partially right. Which led me right into the realization that, once again, I was standing here talking to the guy I liked instead of doing my job. The trip back from the Adirondacks *after* finding the governor would give me plenty of time to ponder my choices. For now, it was time to do my job.

Abruptly, I said, "I'm sorry, but I have to go. I have to fix this. There must be a way."

Quickly I outlined the morning's legislative session, explaining that I had to make things right. As much as I wanted to talk to Steve, to let him comfort me for making a huge mistake, there wasn't time.

When I finished, he said, "Hold on. You're serious. You're crashing the governor's vacation?"

"I have to," I said warily. If he tried to stop me, it would confirm everything Jason said about him. Maybe this was as good a test as any. "As soon as I go home and change."

He nodded. "Okay, then. I'm coming with you."

A wave of relief washed over me. I never should've doubted him. "Really? You don't have to do that. Also, we don't have time to swing by your house, and you can't wear a thousand-dollar suit into the woods."

"No problem. There's a gym bag in my car. I can change at your place."

My heart warmed at his words. Jason was jealous. He was so wrong about this guy. Putting one hand on Steve's cheek, I smiled up at him before placing a soft kiss on his lips. "Thank you so much. I appreciate it."

"Anything for you, sweetheart."

Half an hour later, now dressed for hiking, I was about to climb into my driver's seat when I noticed the front passenger's tire was flat. Lovely. Just what I needed. Unable to believe my terrible luck, I stomped my feet and gritted my teeth and swallowed back a scream when Steve pointed it out.

"It's okay," he said. "We'll take my car. You know where we're going, right?"

With a sigh, I nodded. It wasn't a sign. Just bad luck. Not a major setback. The tire didn't matter, although I wasn't thrilled to have to make time to fix it. We needed to get on the road ASAP.

Steve parked in front of an old, ramshackle RV parked at the end of a dirt road near the lake. Trees lined the path, making the area fairly secluded, although I didn't want to think about how they went anywhere in winter. The decrepit old vehicle didn't look sturdy enough to even make it down the driveway, and the amount of dirt caked around the tires suggested no one had tried since I'd graduated college.

Leaving Steve in the car, I climbed the steps, praying they wouldn't collapse beneath my weight. An unsettling squeak reached my ears, but nothing happened. I knocked, then quickly stepped back onto firm ground.

When the door opened, it took me a minute to recognize Former Senator Tiberius Baker in the man who stood before me. The guy who used to appear on C-SPAN was pale, with short gray hair, tired eyes, and expensive suits. This man glowed with a tan even in early April (probably from the products he sold, now that I thought about it). He looked well-rested and relaxed in a green t-shirt and gloriously soft gray sweatpants.

"Senator Baker?"

He laughed. "Call me Ty. I'm no senator, not anymore. And you are?"

"Oh, right. I'm sorry. My name is Lana Chen. I'm a friend of Curtis's."

"A friend, huh?" He raised his eyebrows. "And also the woman who fell into my empty seat?"

I chuckled. "Guilty. But we are friends now. Your son and I have a surprising amount in common."

Ty turned and walked into the home, gesturing for me to follow. With a start, I realized he was barefoot. There was something unsettling about looking at a former senator's hairy toes. The inside of the RV was nicer than I anticipated, considering the outside. A plush couch lined one wall, a table with two chairs against the other. In the back, a set of stairs led up to a loft presumably containing the bed.

But it made sense that a man who'd lived in luxury for years would make the space available to him as comfortable as possible. He gestured to the couch and offered me a drink, which I declined. I couldn't stay too long, especially with Steve waiting in the car.

"Now, Lana, what can I do for you?"

Quickly, I explained what happened, including how I screwed up and why I needed to find the governor. Even though Ty and I wouldn't have voted the same on most issues had we served at the same time, I used everything in me to appeal to his common decency. To the man who walked away from his entire life when he fell in love. It didn't hurt that Curtis also told me his father used to hate when people snuck clauses in bills that had nothing to do with the primary topic. A deplorable tactic, he'd called it.

When I finished, Ty shook his head. "What are they thinking? I tell you, sometimes, I swear the party has lost its damn mind. That's why I walked away. I'm glad Curtis didn't win my seat. Please don't tell him that, by the way. But my boy could do much better."

"It's possible he wanted to help make a change from the inside."

"Beating his head against a brick wall, that's what he'd be doing," he said. "He should've run as himself, and not as the person he thought his mother wanted him to be."

I nodded. "If he had, I wouldn't be in this mess, so I tend to agree. Do you think you can help me?"

"Help you find Governor Abbot's campsite? Sure. I've been there dozens of times."

For the first time in hours, I breathed a sigh of relief. "Thank you so much. There are no words for how much I appreciate this."

"We didn't have GPS in my day," he said. "We had to find stuff the old-fashioned way. By looking."

My heart sank. "You can't tell me how to get there? I don't suppose you'd be willing to take me?"

"No offense, young lady, but of course not. I'm done with politics, and that includes lobbying the governor, no matter how good the cause." He walked over to a side table and opened a drawer. A moment later, he turned back to me and held something out. "Do you know what this is?"

It was on the tip of my tongue to ask if he thought I was a child, but getting snarky with the only person who could help me wasn't likely to be useful. Instead, I nodded. "Yeah. My dad was in the Air Force. He loved maps. Hung them all over his office."

"Air Force, huh? How'd you wind up here? No Air Force bases in New York."

"My grandparents live in the area. After Dad retired, he got a job as a pilot with one of the smaller airports. Still loves maps, though," I added, hoping to get the conversation back on track.

"Right. Okay." He led me to the table and unfolded the paper, showing a maze of lines and grids and pencil marks and pen. The map was faded along the fold lines, making me wonder if it was the same piece of paper he'd used to take Curtis camping in the nineties. "Now, I can't give you my only map, but I can show you where to go."

"No problem." I whipped out my phone and opened the video camera. "Just show me the route, and I'll follow you."

"Huh. Are you sure about that?"

"Of course I'm sure. This will be way better than drawing my own."

"Don't blame me if you get lost, that's all I have to say." Ty hunched over the table and traced a thick, black line with his finger. "If you were taking a camper, there's a longer way in. Paved, smooth, a pleasant drive. But it'll add time to your trip. Hiking from the dirt road is much faster."

"No trailer," I said. "I'm not afraid to hike it."

Five minutes later, I had a video detailing where Governor Abbot should be, and a debt of gratitude I would never be able to repay. "Thank you so much, Mr. Baker. Is there anything I can do for you?"

"Well, now that you mention it…" His sharp gaze zeroed in on my skin, the flaky dry patches and the oily bits. "How are you doing for moisturizer?"

Ten minutes later I returned to the car, having spent a couple hundred dollars to procure a bag of products guaranteed to make my face feel "naked." Since I normally didn't wear clothes on my face, I had no idea what he meant, but either way, the expense would be worth it if we found the governor. Besides, who couldn't use more skincare products? Winters were long here, and too much heat was drying.

Steve's eyes bulged. "Did you buy his entire stash?"

"Hush." I handed him a jar. "Here. This will help reduce your pores and unleash your, um… what does it say?"

"My inner moon goddess?"

"Right. Happy birthday," I said. "Let's go."

He started the car and backed in a circle to pull out onto the main road. "You shouldn't have. Really. Especially because my birthday was last month."

"Fine, then, I'll keep it. It's a souvenir of the weirdest day ever."

"Weird isn't always bad. We've got all afternoon to ourselves now."

The thought of several hours alone with Steve, nothing to do but get to know each other better and drive and walk through the woods, made me smile for the first time all day. "Thank you so much for coming with me. I'm sure you had better things to do today."

He reached over and squeezed my knee. Our eyes met briefly, and a slow smile spread across his face. "It's my pleasure. I'm excited to get to spend time with you."

If he played his cards right, there could be plenty of pleasure ahead for both of us. And he seemed to have a winning hand. But one thing at a time.

First, I needed to find the governor. Then I needed to convince her to veto the bill she'd championed from the beginning. And I still had no idea how I was going to do it.

Chapter Thirteen

Two hours later, I revised my assessment of the entire mission. My initial inclination that this was a ludicrous task had been kind. Useless, pointless, a total waste of time—those were all more accurate descriptions.

Recent rain had left the path muddy in places and without proper hiking boots, I was slipping and sliding all over the place. Twice Steve jumped and screamed at a rustling in the bushes that turned out to be nothing more than birds. Or even his imagination. It took everything in me not to roll my eyes at him. Silly city boy.

We were never going to find Governor Abbot out here. Worse, her annual retreat hid in the heart of the Adirondacks which, although beautiful, were not equipped with Wi-Fi. My GPS was useless. My phone was useless. The video Ty made wasn't nearly as helpful as I'd expected, because so much had changed since his map was printed three thousand years ago. Apparently they'd rebuilt some of the paths entirely, because at one point we made a turn and nearly toppled into a ravine.

My sense of direction sucked. Shockingly, Steve's was even worse.

"How did you go your whole life without knowing how to navigate using the sun?"

He shrugged. "I grew up in Manhattan. I never saw the sun."

Since the woods were undeniably not laid out in a grid, and we couldn't hail a taxi to take us to our destination, I decided to shut up and focus on the path. A good idea, it turned out, since my legs nearly went out from under me. Freaking mud. More than once, I found myself using my strength and core stability to grab onto branches to stay upright. Thank you, pole fitness. Who said those skills didn't translate to real life?

Finally, we came to a fork in the road. Steve swore it would get us back on the right track after watching the video on my phone about six times. He took me to the right. We passed a very-familiar giant rock before coming into a large clearing. A clearing that, if I wasn't mistaken, we'd passed through when we first arrived. The same fallen log lay across one side, looking even more tempting as a place to stop and rest than the first time I saw it.

I looked from the log to my phone to Steve and back again. Fork me. If I was right, we'd lost at least an hour wandering around with no clue where we were going.

"Oh, hashtag. Did we walk in a giant circle?"

"Of course not. What are you talking about?"

I pointed to a giant tree split with lightning. "We passed this when we got here. Look, there's a bird's nest on the third branch up. Mama bird was here earlier."

He shook his head. "No, listen. I figured it out. We're almost there. We need to go to the right."

Pulling out my phone, I shook it as if that would magically get me a signal again. It didn't, but Ty's video started playing again. Instead of following Steve, I watched the entire thing from the beginning.

"No, look. We're not remotely near where we're supposed

to be. In fact…" I squinted through the trees. "I think we're about fifty feet from the parking lot. Look. That tree's in the way, but I'm pretty sure that's your car."

Steve came up behind me, his breath hot against my neck. "Lana, listen. I promise, we're where we should be. Come here."

His arms wrapped around my waist, pulling me against his chest. The temptation to lean back was strong, but we were on a mission. We were also lost in the forest. Well, lost in the sense that we had no idea where to go. I could see where we'd parked the car. Either way, we were at least another hour away from finding Governor Abbot, and it was after three. I didn't know how long it would take to talk to Governor Abbot or how much light we'd have left when we found her. Which meant no time for making out in the woods.

Well, okay, maybe a little time. As Steve's lips traced a path up my neck, I swooned. Turning in his arms, I raised my face to his. Kissing did relax me. And at the moment, I desperately needed to calm down before we continued.

His hands moved down my back to my waist, and I tensed up. "What's wrong?"

"Nothing's wrong, per se," I said. "But we can't be doing this. Not here. We have to go."

"Come on. Everything is going to be okay. Let's take advantage of this beautiful day and our time away from the office."

Jason's voice from earlier cut through my head again. A sinking feeling filled my gut as I once again thought about all the things he'd said. "Hold on. Steve, what is going on here?"

He smiled at me, all innocence and charm. "What are you talking about? I want to enjoy this time alone with my girl."

My heart jumped at his words, but my brain quickly shushed it. Something very strange was happening, and I needed to get to the bottom of it. "Are you trying to stop me from getting to Governor Abbot?"

He started to argue, then raised his hands and dropped them as if engaging in a mental argument. "You know what? This is a waste of time. Yeah, I don't want you to find Abbot. I worked hard on this bill, and I'm not about to let you ruin everything at the last minute."

I gasped. One hand went to my mouth. "Fork me. Jason was right. This is your bill. And you never told me."

"Of course not. If you knew it was my bill, you'd want to hear all about what was in it, and then I'd have to lie. It was so much easier to distract you and let you screw up on your own."

With every word out of his mouth, Steve became more of a monster. I couldn't believe I'd ever found him attractive. I couldn't believe he would do this to me. Every moment we spent together was a lie. Every kiss, every look. I wanted to throw up. Literally the only thing that saved me from losing my lunch was at least knowing my gut stopped me from sleeping with him. Every time my resolve started to crumble, something told me to wait. Now I knew why.

"Get the hell away from me," I said.

"With pleasure," he replied. "People only deal with you because they want to see the stripper who stumbled into politics. Now that I've gotten your vote, I don't need you."

I bit my tongue so hard, copper filled my mouth. Since my first day on the job, I had ignored the stripper comments. My past didn't matter, I deserved respect whether I was a stripper or not. Personally, I loved the idea of getting different perspectives in the legislature. We should vote in a stripper, a plumber, a bookstore owner, immigrants from all over the world, religious scholars. For the state to prosper, we needed different viewpoints. It was one reason I took the job when Mel suggested it—there was an appalling lack of diversity in the chamber.

But the fact that Steve spent all this time pretending he didn't look down on me made my blood boil. I never should've gotten involved with him.

"You used me." He didn't deny it. I cursed under my breath. "I can't believe I ever thought you were a decent guy."

"And I can't believe I never got you to give it up. If I'd had any idea how much time I would waste pretending to care about the things you talk about, I'd have bought some good earplugs. Or found another way to get my votes." He turned to go.

I watched for a minute before words came to me. I couldn't let him leave without knowing. "Tell me why. It's one bill. How important can it be?"

"Your question only proves how little you understand," he said. "It's one bill that will affect property values now and in the future. My clients will make a killing once it's signed, and now so will I."

"So it was all money."

"Not all. Who doesn't want to bang a stripper?"

My blood boiled. "You're disgusting. Jason was right."

"You're not a senator, Lana, you're a joke."

The trees parted, and he pushed his way onto an adjacent path. Ahead of him, as I suspected sat his car. Jerk. My first instinct was to race after him, block his path, and scream at him until I ran out of words.

But it wasn't worth it. Steve didn't want to help me, only wanted to get into my pants. Even if I could shame him into coming back—why bother? I didn't particularly want to spend any more time in his company. Although, come to think of it, he was my ride home. I'd need him to at least drive me to a place where I could get reception to call Mel.

In the distance, a door slammed, cutting off my words. An engine roared to life. Tires squealed. Then silence. I was too late.

Just like that, he was gone.

What a weasel. I couldn't believe Steve ditched me in the middle of the forest, with nothing but a video of a map on my phone to guide my way. I mean, okay, on the edge of the parking lot, but we were still miles from the main road.

It would take me ages to hike out of here—assuming I could figure out which roads to take. Mountain paths weren't exactly direct.

Not knowing what else to do, I sank to a log and pulled out my phone. In the video, everything Ty said seemed so clear. The map made perfect sense while he was explaining it. However, now that I was here, with trees blocking my view of most of the paths, nothing made any sense. I'd be better off using the compass on my phone to find the highway and starting over, but I wasn't ready to give up yet.

This was stupid. Governor Abbot could be anywhere. I still didn't know how to talk her into my way of thinking once I found her. My entire plan assumed she didn't call the police the moment I crashed her vacation. I needed to know what to say before I got there, because I wouldn't have much time.

I could ask for help? Maybe that would work. What if I pretended to be lost? If Governor Abbot were extremely distracted or hungover, she might fall for it.

With a sigh, I lowered my head into my hands. What a terrible idea. What was I even doing here? One tear streaked down my cheek, then another. I was running out of time, and I knew it, but I didn't have the energy to get up. All the fight went out of me when Steve called me a joke and walked away.

This entire excursion had been a colossal mistake.

Chapter Fourteen

The sound of my name pulled me out of my misery. Not because anyone was actually talking to me, but because I realized it would be dark in a couple of hours, and then I'd be wandering the forest with no camping gear, no food, and nothing but my slowly dying phone for light. I needed to make my way back to the road so I could call for help, especially now that I'd started hearing things that weren't there.

With a groan, I stood up and stretched, cursing the cold for making me so stiff while I sulked. Then I heard it again.

"Lana?"

Yup, I was hallucinating. Although, if I were hallucinating that someone would brave the cold to come rescue me, the voice in my head would belong to Riz Ahmed. This voice sounded a lot like—

"Lana? Are you there?"

"Jason? Jason!"

I bounded to my feet and raced toward the sound, not even trying to hide the happiness and relief on my face. I didn't know why he was here, and I didn't care. A moment later, he rounded a turn in the path and stepped into view. I catapulted into his arms.

"Lana! Thank goodness," he said. "I thought I'd never find you."

"What are you doing here? Are you a mirage?"

He chuckled and set me back on my feet. "No. I'm real. I came to get you. There's a huge storm coming in tonight. It's not safe to be out here. You'll have to look for the Governor tomorrow."

"You know, that's way above and beyond your duties as Welcome Wagon."

"Oddly enough, saving your life isn't in the Legislative Mentor Handbook." He swallowed. "I'd like to think that, before our argument earlier, we were becoming friends."

Friends. What a beautiful word. "Definitely. But still, driving two hours north? I have a map. If things had gone as planned, I'd be on my way back right now."

He shuffled his feet and avoided my gaze. "Sometimes I get feelings about things…"

"Come on, what gives?" I asked. "It's been one hell of a day, and I'm all done with people I trusted lying to me."

At that, he finally met my eyes. "I overheard a few guys talking in the cafeteria about how Steve canceled an afternoon meeting because he needed to 'go into the woods or something.' I put two and two together." He paused. "Look, I know you don't want to hear anything bad about Steve, but—"

"You were right. I was wrong."

"What happened?"

I shook my head. "Not now. Incidentally, I appreciate you coming to my rescue, especially after the things I said earlier. I also appreciate the lack of 'I told you so.'"

He grinned. "I just got here. Give me a second."

I snort-laughed at that. "How did you know? He told me

you didn't like him because you both liked the same girl, and you never got over her picking him."

"Ha!" A bellow of laughter escaped him. "Oh, that's rich. That's what he said?"

"Yeah. Why?"

"He slept with my ex-wife."

I gasped. "While you were married?"

"Yup."

"And he knew—?"

"He knew."

"Holy fork." Jason shot me a quizzical look, which brought me back to reality. This wasn't the time to talk about my no-swearing pact or ask my burning questions about his previously-unrevealed marriage. "We'll come back to that when we have more time. How did you find me?"

Jason looked at the ground and scratched the back of his head. "I, uh, asked Melody to track your GPS coordinates."

My eyes narrowed as my hands went to my hips. "Excuse me?"

"I know, I know, a total violation of your privacy," he said.

"She has that access for emergencies!"

"This is an emergency!" He gestured at the sky. "In about twenty minutes, we're going to be stuck here."

At his words, I paused in my righteous indignation and looked around. I'd thought the trees here blocked the light, but we stood near a clearing. Ominous clouds hovered in the sky, much too close for comfort. A frigid breeze made the hair on my arms stand up.

"Please tell me I'm looking at a lot of pollen in the air."

"I wish I could," Jason said. "But that appears to be snow. Big flakes, coming down fast. In April. Oh, man. Who would've thought?"

"I would love to answer your question, but I'm afraid my

phone has no service. Remind me to check Google when we get back to civilization."

"Step one: let's get back to civilization first. I'm sorry I invaded your privacy."

I glanced up at the rapidly darkening sky and the snow already starting to stick to the forest floor. "Oh, right. You're forgiven. Thank you for coming to my rescue. Let's go."

"After you." He made a sweeping bow, then paused and looked around. "What happened to Steve? He's not still here, is he? We can't leave him in the woods. Even if he is a jerk."

I grumbled to myself, but of course Jason was right. I didn't want Steve to freeze to death. Well, okay, I like twelve percent wanted it. "Jerk ditched me. He's probably halfway back to Albany by now. He drove away about an hour ago. Unless you passed a broken-down BMW your way in, he's fine. But we can call him once we get to a place with reception."

"Okay. Let's go before we need to dig my car out."

Jason led me back to the parking lot. After our last conversation, I'd been worried he hated me. It was nice to see we could still be friends, even after I'd screwed everything up. And he apparently didn't hold my terrible taste in men against me.

Hold on. My feet skidded to a halt.

"What's wrong?" Jason asked.

"Governor Abbot. She's out there somewhere. She has no idea what's coming."

He took my arm when I would've bolted back into the forest. "She's fine. I talked to her Chief of Staff on my way in. They called her security detail on the satellite phone, and she's being extracted now by people far better equipped to find her than we are."

I breathed a sigh of relief. "Thank you so much for everything. I still need to talk to her, though. Convince her not to sign the bill."

"Not tonight, you don't." Fat flakes started to drop from the sky. "We need to go if you want to make it home in one piece."

Inside the forest, we'd been somewhat sheltered from the full extent of the storm. Away from the tree cover, the snow had started to stick. A thin coating covered the pavement, and the icy air sent a chill down my spine. I regretted not grabbing something warmer to wear. Then again, if I had, my "I'm not arguing, I'm explaining why I'm right" sweatshirt would be enjoying a ride home with Steve right now.

Jason remotely started his car as soon as we got within range. A glance at the space where Steve parked earlier made my blood pressure rise, but he wasn't worth another thought unless we happened to find him stranded by the side of the road somewhere. I could dream.

The parking lot wasn't far from the highway, but windy, unpaved paths covered with snow didn't make for the smoothest travel. Jason hunched over the wheel, focused on the road. Since conversation wasn't an option, I tried to get a signal to text Mel and thank her for her role in saving me.

When we finally made a left turn onto the paved road leading to the highway, Jason heaved a sigh and leaned back against the seat. His grip on the wheel loosened as he signaled for the turn onto the on-ramp. The tension drained from my shoulders. I hadn't even realized how high my shoulders had gotten until my back unclenched.

"Any signal?" Jason asked. "I'd like to see how bad the weather is up ahead."

"Nothing yet." I held my device against the roof of the car as if that would magically fix everything, but we were still miles from any cell towers. This part of the highway had emergency telephones set up every two miles for stranded motorists. "If you want to pull over at a call box, I can try Mel."

He shook his head. "No, better to keep going."

We made it about five miles before my phone finally

beeped with a message, letting me know it had connected to a tower. Unfortunately, the words on the screen didn't make me feel any better. "Uh-oh."

"What's wrong?" Jason asked, eyes not leaving the road.

"It's an alert," I said. "There's an accident ahead. A big rig skidded out, turned sideways, and flipped. Southbound I-87 is closed at Lake George, traffic backed up for miles. We need to get off the highway, or we'll be sitting there all night."

"Got it. Thanks."

We drove in silence as the snow continued to fall. I didn't want to distract Jason's focus on the road, but also, with him driving, it was on me to figure out how to get home. I searched around for alternate routes, but it didn't take long to realize it would be safer to pull over somewhere and wait out the storm. Back roads weren't a paving priority, and I strongly suspected Jason's nice-but-not-flashy sedan didn't have four-wheel drive. Also, I hadn't eaten in several hours.

As soon as I finished the thought, my stomach let out a howl. How embarrassing. I wanted to die on the spot. Jason's eyes slid over to me briefly, but to his credit, he didn't comment.

"We should stop," he finally said. "Find a diner and hole up. It's getting worse, I can barely see the road, and the last thing I want is to sit in traffic with a hundred other cars on a closed highway in a blizzard."

"Agreed."

A sign informed us that the nearest restaurant would be two exits up the road, which was longer than I wanted to stay where we were. Unfortunately, my phone confirmed we weren't likely to find food anywhere within ten miles of the closer exit, and I preferred not to go wandering off into the middle of nowhere. Better chance of someone coming by to do a quick plowing and salting before we headed home.

At the end of the off-ramp, a sign told us we'd find food

and lodging to the right, gas to the left. A slight overstatement. To the right, we found a closed diner attached to a small hotel.

"No food." I sighed. "We might as well keep going."

Jason pulled into a parking spot and shut off the engine. "Sorry, but I need a break."

"That's fine." I gestured to the building in front of us. "Let's go see if they can direct us somewhere that might still be open. Then I'll drive."

"You go ahead. I'll wait here." He leaned his head back against the seat rest, closing his eyes. Immediately, I felt terrible. He was exhausted because he had to drop everything to come rescue me in a blizzard.

If I hadn't voted for that stupid bill, or if I hadn't decided to bring Steve of all people with me, none of this would've happened. All I had to do was read the revised version, but I believed Steve when he said it was no big deal. The fact that Jason had been entirely right about my crush only made me feel worse.

There had been no reason in the world not to trust Jason's opinion. Or at least have a conversation with him. What do they say? Trust, but verify? I consulted Google approximately six hundred times a day, yet I couldn't be bothered to do any research at all the smooth-talker with the sexy crooked smile.

The more I thought about it, the more I couldn't believe Jason hadn't left me to rot in the woods. Or at least spit out one or two "I told you so"s. I didn't deserve such a good friend. Before going inside, I reached over and touched his arm.

"Thank you. Really."

"Don't mention it."

An icy blast hit me the second the car door opened. My feet skidded on the snow. At least I was wearing sneakers instead of heels or ballet flats, but they weren't waterproof. My feet instantly went numb. The ten feet from the car to the front doors of the hotel felt like miles. When I finally made it, I wanted to fall down on the ground and kiss the carpet.

The lobby was small, yet cozy. A fireplace divided the room into two parts. The "hotel" part with the check-in desk and elevators on one side, a more inviting seating area on the other. A massive couch covered in blue and pink floral print sat facing a television mounted above the fireplace. Light from the flames flickered off the hearth. I was about two seconds from throwing myself in front of it before I realized we were on the ground floor of a multistory building, and the fireplace was in the middle of the room. There was no exit for smoke, and also, the thing gave off zero heat. Fake.

Behind the desk stood a teenage girl with a long red ponytail. She looked young to be manning the desk on her own in a blizzard, but maybe that wasn't intentional. Also, I sucked at guessing people's ages. She could be forty for all I knew.

"Hi! I'm Abby. Can I help you?"

Rubbing my hands together for warmth, I stepped closer to the desk, away from the doors. "I don't suppose the diner is going to open for dinner any time soon?"

She shook her head, ponytail swishing from side to side. "Sorry. Normally we open at four, but it's not happening tonight. My mom's the cook, and she's stuck at home."

"Do you know somewhere else I could get a bite to eat?"

"Glen's Falls?" She named a small town not remotely near our location.

"Thanks, but I was hoping for something a little closer."

"Sorry." She shrugged. "I think the gas station is still open."

Wonderful. Gas station food in a blizzard. Any port in a storm, sure, but Jason deserved better. Poor guy looked so exhausted. I couldn't imagine telling him he needed to eat gas station food while sitting in his car.

"Look, I probably shouldn't tell you this," Abby said, "but it's going to be a slow night. We offer room service for guests."

"Even when the diner is closed?"

"Not normally, but I know how to make a few things. If you want to check in, I can bring a burger and fries up to your room."

Right then, no food had even sounded more delicious. My mouth watered at the thought of biting into a thick, juicy cheeseburger. Oh, and what if they had bacon? Salty deliciousness… I got so lost in the imagery, I almost forgot Abby was waiting for a response.

"Yes, thank you, that sounds wonderful," I said. "I'll take a room until the storm passes."

"Lucky you, you get it all night. We don't rent rooms by the hour. Double or King?"

It didn't matter in the slightest, as long as we could sit while we ate. We wouldn't be sleeping in it. "Uh, King, I guess."

"Excellent choice. The only available double has a leaky toilet. Name?"

Moments later, I held a key card in my hand, Abby had my credit card, and she promised to deliver two meals to the room as soon as possible. Feeling better for the first time in hours, I went back outside to the parking lot to get Jason.

The empty parking lot.

While I'd been inside booking a room, Jason had left me. Ditched by two different men in the same day.

What a nightmare.

Chapter Fifteen

For a long moment, I stood in the parking lot, watching giant flakes fill in the tire tracks Jason's car had made in the snow. I couldn't believe he'd leave me here. Was this his plan? Get me to a safe location and then bail? Sure, I could get home in the morning, but—what a creep. I'd thought he'd forgiven me for not listening to him about Steve (not to mention screwing up the vote), but clearly, I didn't know anything about Jason. Anyone who would do this to me wasn't a friend.

A tear tracked down my face, cutting an icy path down to my chin.

Shivers racked my body, and I realized I could curse Jason's name and cry about my terrible luck inside as well as out here. Preferably while eating *his* hamburger. As I turned to go, movement caught the corner of my eye. Headlights swept the parking lot. Between the low light and the snow, I couldn't tell much other than that it was a moving vehicle. I assumed Abby still had rooms, so they were in luck. Hopefully they were having a better day than me.

The car pulled to a stop in front of me. A parking brake cranked into place, and then the door swung open.

"Hey. What are you doing out here?" Jason peered closer at my face, taking in the tear streaks and my red eyes. "Are you okay?"

"I thought you'd left me here." To my dismay, my voice cracked. I sniffled, not trusting myself to say anymore.

"Oh, Lana, I'm so sorry," he said. "Didn't you get my text?"

I shook my head. After handing over my credit card and booking the room, I'd come right outside to get him. It hadn't occurred to me to check my phone.

He wrapped his arms around me, and I put my head on his shoulder. A combination of relief and exhaustion caused the flood of tears I'd barely been holding back to let loose. Jason rubbed my back, offering me comfort both from my terrible day and the storm.

He murmured in my ear. "I would never leave you. The radio said the storm is going to get worse, and it could take hours to clear the highway. I saw you talking to the girl inside, and she started typing—it looked like you'd decided to take a room. Since we can't go anywhere, and we don't have any provisions, I went to the gas station. It's all in my message."

"I didn't know. I—I—"

He pulled back, wiping my tears away. "I'm not Steve. I wouldn't abandon you."

I sniffled. Having him see me at my lowest point on top of everything else killed me. I couldn't imagine what he must think of me. "Thank you. I'm sorry. It's been a terrible day."

"Well, it's about to get better." He reached into the car and pulled out a plastic bag. "Who's got FUNYUNS?!"

A chuckle escaped me. "I'll see your FUNYUNS and raise you a cheeseburger with fries. Abby's making them for us inside."

"I don't know who Abby is, but I want to marry her."

"She looks about sixteen."

"I will settle for the burger." He slammed the door shut and gestured to the front door with an overemphasized bow. "After you."

Following the instructions Abby had given me, I soon found Room 4. The door swung open to reveal a small, reasonably clean room. It wasn't fancy, but looked comfortable. To the right, double-mirrored closet doors showed that I looked every bit as terrible as expected. Red eyes gazed dully out of my face. The few traces of makeup from this morning that hadn't been cried away were smudged all over my face, streaking toward my ears. My hair resembled a bird's nest. Inches from the giant mirror, I now saw what Ty meant about my "flaky patches" and "danger zones." Too bad my couple hundreds of dollars' worth of skincare products were still in Steve's car.

Across from the closet was a closed door I assumed led to a bathroom. One of those very loud-patterned spreads designed to hide stains covered the king-sized bed. The room also contained two nightstands, a dresser with a giant TV on top, a firm-looking couch, a small desk, and a single chair. Not the worst place to spend a few hours. Far better than, say, sitting on a log in the forest in a snowstorm.

Our food hadn't arrived yet, so I took a moment to explore Jason's booty from the gas station. Two toothbrushes, a can of spray deodorant, fuzzy socks, and two giant t-shirts. One said "Life is Good, Take it Easy" and the other said "Keep it Simple" with a picture of a monkey lounging in a chair.

"I wouldn't have thought these were your style," I said.

He flushed. "It was all they had. I didn't know your size, but I figured for sleeping, bigger was better. Less restrictive."

A smile stretched across my face at his thoughtfulness. "Thank you so much. Do you have a preference?"

"Personally, I like 'Life is Easy,' but I'm flexible."

There were so many directions I could go with that comment, but a knock on the door prevented me from having to choose. Jason went to open it, and a moment later, Abby wheeled a cart into the room. The smell of hot fries and beef and melty cheese made my mouth water.

"If you don't need anything else, I'll see you in the morning," she said. "Breakfast starts at six."

"Oh, we won't be here long," Jason said, leaning toward her. He moved so smoothly, I didn't even see the tip until money appeared in Abby's hand. "Once the storm clears, we'll be on our way."

She shrugged. "K. Thanks."

In my current state, I couldn't even wait for the door to close behind her before I dove for the dinner tray. Since I didn't know what Jason liked on his burger, I'd had Abby put all the possible fixings on the side. The amount of tomatoes, lettuce, and onion spilling over the edge of the plate, for a moment, I thought she'd given us a salad.

Snagging a fry, I took a bite. A moan escaped me. After hours of wandering lost in the woods, then driving around in the snow, it was the most amazing thing I'd ever held in my mouth.

"Should I leave the two of you alone?" Jason asked.

His voice broke into my thoughts. For a moment, I'd almost forgotten he was there. "Huh?"

"You seem to be having a good time with that French fry."

My cheeks grew warm. "Sorry. I just realized how hungry I am."

"No, I'm sorry. It's nice to see someone enjoying food, that's all. I didn't mean to make you feel bad. Look." Leaning forward, he grabbed a fry from the plate closest to him and stuffed it into his mouth. "On second thought, maybe you should leave *me* alone. These are delicious."

"Not a chance."

I picked up one of the plates. "I'll take this one? They're both the same."

"Not true," he said. "At the moment, your plate has more fries. I may have to fight you for it."

"I wouldn't do that if I were you," I said. "I may be small, but I'm strong."

Jason picked up the other plate and gestured toward the couch. "Better not risk it."

We ate in companionable silence for a long time. The urge to dive face-first into my plate and gobble everything in sight was strong, but we had at least an hour before the storm slowed and even longer before the highway reopened. Might as well savor my food.

And maybe take a nap.

Once we'd piled the dishes back on the room service tray and wheeled it out to the hallway, I yawned and stretched. "What do you think? Want to rest a bit before we get back on the road? I'm beat."

He glanced toward the closed curtains for a moment, then back at me. "Resting is a good idea, but for longer than you're expecting. I don't see being able to drive in an hour or two."

"It's OK. If you're too tired, I can drive once I rest a bit."

"It's not that. Look outside."

"You don't think it's going to let up?" To be honest, I was far from a snow expert, but I was trying to look at the bright side. It was April. April snow wasn't supposed to be a thing. Even though it was happening at that very moment.

In answer to my question, Jason shook his head. He tapped on his phone several times, then studied the screen. He even turned it back and forth a few times, which seemed like a bad sign. I had no idea how to read a storm tracker, but if he thought turning it upside-down would help, the outlook was pretty bad. "Sorry, Lana. We're not going anywhere tonight. It's getting worse."

"Really? I thought it was supposed to pass quickly."

"That's what they were saying at lunch, but not now. Go look."

I went to the curtains covering the far wall and pulled them open. A sea of whiteness glared back at me, so blinding I wished I'd worn sunglasses.

"It's not safe out there," Jason said.

As much as I wanted to argue, I knew when I was beaten. Leaving the safety of the hotel would be an enormous mistake. "Yeah. I'm so sorry. I hope you didn't have plans tonight."

"It's fine. I'll go book my own room."

Not the way I'd planned to spend my evening. Seemed silly to rent a hotel room less than fifty miles from home, but it beat crashing and dying on the way home.

I sighed. "Since it was my bright idea to come out here without checking the weather report, your room is on me."

"Don't be silly. I'll pay for my own."

"No, really. I insist."

"Well, I insist harder," he said.

I wanted to argue with him, I did. But more than that, I wanted to strip the nasty bedspread off the king-sized bed beside me, crawl under the covers, and sleep for the next ten hours. I didn't have the energy to race Jason to the lobby and see who could hand Abby a credit card faster. Maybe she'd let me switch the cards in the morning.

With a yawn, I slipped out of my shoes. "Okay, fine. But you'll have to let me make it up to you when we get home."

"Deal." His tone suggested he didn't mean it, but that was an argument for another day. "You're asleep on your feet. I'm going to head out."

"Are you sure? It's early." Jason found me in the woods around three. Even considering how long it took us to get to the hotel, it couldn't be much past six or six-thirty.

"Yeah. I'm tired, too," he said. "Besides, my briefcase is in the car. I've got some work I can do."

Right. Work. The thing that brought us out here in the first place. He was missing out on a day's worth of important stuff because I'd been impulsive and short-sighted. Of course he didn't want to spend any more time with me. He had to be barely containing his fury.

Biting my lip, I nodded. "Right. I'll see you in the morning. Text me when you wake up."

"No problem." Jason grabbed the bag he'd picked up at the gas station and removed half the items, stacking them on the dresser.

When the door shut behind him, my shoulders sagged. He was right. I was exhausted. Mentally, emotionally, spiritually. A long night's sleep would do me good. After a shower.

As tired as I was, I couldn't climb into bed without one, not after wandering the woods all afternoon. To be honest, the fact that I hadn't showered before eating only proved how hungry I must've been.

The scalding water beating against my skin felt amazing. I never wanted to get out. But eventually, a banging drew my attention. What now? Were the neighbors fighting? Enjoying the heck out of their room?

Please, please don't let the hotel be on fire.

Leaning over, I stuck my head out of the shower curtain and opened the bathroom door a crack. Naturally, no one was there. No one had a key. But now I could clearly hear knocking on my outer door. Also hear a voice on the other side of the door, calling my name.

"Jason?"

If he responded, I couldn't tell. Jumping out of the shower, I wrapped a towel around myself. Hotel towels were ridiculously small, but I wasn't super tall. It covered what it needed to, barely. Swiping a lock of wet black hair out of my eyes, I went to the door.

"Jason? What's wrong?"

"Can you open the door, please? I don't want to have to yell."

Right. I glanced down at my dripping body, barely covered with the towel, and sighed. As friendly as we were becoming, I couldn't greet him in a hotel room without any clothes on. That was so far beyond professional, even in an emergency, I couldn't do it. "Give me two minutes to get dressed."

I toweled off as quickly as I could, grabbing the t-shirt Jason had left and pulling it over my head, then looked around. Obviously he hadn't gotten me underwear at the gas station—and I wouldn't have worn them if he did because that's weird. Before getting into the shower, I'd rinsed out the pair I'd been wearing earlier, intending to flip them inside out and put them on in the morning after they dried. Now, I couldn't bring myself to step into still-damp panties.

Oh, well. At least the t-shirt hit my knees.

When I swung the door open, Jason stood holding his phone. "One minute, fifty-seven seconds. Impressive."

"I'm a woman of my word," I said. "What's up?"

"Nice monkey." At the confused look on my face, he clarified. "The shirt."

"Oh, right. Thanks."

"Sorry to do this, but can I come in? Abby's not down there. A sign on the front desk says she's taking her dinner break. I'll try again in an hour or so."

Although I desperately wanted to crawl into bed and go to sleep, I couldn't leave him to wait in the hall alone for the lobby to reopen. "Sure, no problem."

"You're the best." He stepped into the room, shutting the door behind him. "Do you want to watch a movie?"

I did not. I wanted to go to sleep. But if we didn't turn on the TV, the alternative was to talk, and I was much too tired to make conversation. So I handed him the remote, told him to turn on anything but political news, and settled onto the bed. Then I looked at Jason and hesitated. The bed was a million times more comfortable than the sofa or the chair. We were only friends. And yet....

Hanging out on a hotel room bed with my mentor wearing only a t-shirt was seriously unprofessional.

A voice in the back of my head spoke up. *No one would ever know.*

I would know.

And yet... he'd driven a hundred miles to save me. I'd gotten him stranded. He had no bed because of me. I couldn't make him sit on the floor. Or the rock hard sofa. And I was much too tired to move.

It would be fine. Friends could watch a movie together.

Finally, as the silence was starting to become awkward, I patted the other side of the bed. "Want to sit?"

"You don't mind?"

"Just take your shoes off," I said. "You can see the TV better from here."

Jason left his loafers by the door, then settled onto the bed beside me. We had a king-sized bed, so we could easily stretch out without touching. To be honest, the mattress was so big, we probably didn't need to rent a separate room for Jason. Not when the goal was to go to sleep, then leave first thing in the morning.

On the other hand, separate rooms helped maintain a professional distance. People would talk when we both missed work tomorrow. I didn't want anything to fuel the flames of gossip. Also, I didn't have clean pants or underwear, so using separate rooms wasn't the worst idea. Suddenly uncomfortably aware of my partial nudity, I grabbed the remote and pointed it at the screen to give me anything else to focus on.

The storm had apparently taken out the satellite, because we couldn't get any channels to load. After flipping around the dial, I gave up and threw the remote onto the couch, leaning back against the headboard.

"Are you ready to talk?" Jason asked. "You never told me what happened with Steve."

I shook my head. "Let's just say, you were right about him, and I was an idiot."

"No, you're not. You are far from the first woman to be charmed by a sweet-talking jerk. Or even by that sweet-talking jerk."

Right. I couldn't believe Jason's ex-wife had an affair with Steve. No wonder he didn't like the guy. I only wished he'd told me earlier. "Is that supposed to make me feel better?"

"You know, in my head, I thought it would, yet I can see where I miscalculated." He leaned over and squeezed my hand. "Hey, it's okay. Don't beat yourself up. You're new to the legislature. I should've warned you earlier. By the time I tried to say something—"

"—I'd already fallen under his spell?"

"I was going to say my approach left much to be desired."

"Thanks."

I was so tired. He looked so warm and inviting, sitting beside me. I leaned over to give him a hug, yet somehow it turned into me resting my head against his shoulder. I shouldn't. We worked together.

Working with Steve never bothered me.

I never stopped to think about why I shouldn't be involved with Steve. That was half the reason we were here. If I had, I'd have realized immediately he was a distraction, not the right choice.

Before I could talk myself into moving back to my side of the bed, Jason put his arm around me. I nestled closer against his side. He felt safe, warm. "You're a good friend."

"I should see if Abby's back at the desk so I can book my own room," he said. "You're wiped out."

"Don't go yet," I said. "Stay with me?"

Our eyes met. Something shifted between us. I don't know how or why it happened, but in the moment, we weren't co-workers, stranded in a snowstorm after a poorly-timed road trip. Something more lingered beneath the surface, close enough for either of us to grab it. I knew he shouldn't stay, but I didn't want him to leave.

"You know I can't. That doesn't mean I don't want to."

Disappointment thickened my voice. "I know."

Jason smiled at me before leaning back against the head-board. "But I can stay until you fall asleep."

The gesture made me feel safe. Not all men were Steves. There were still plenty of good ones out there. Jason gave me hope that maybe, once we unraveled this mess I'd made, I could find someone who liked me for me and not what I could do for him.

Or maybe, I thought, as my eyes fluttered shut, I already had.

Chapter Sixteen

The next morning dawned bright and clear. I woke up and stretched, reveling in the clean-feeling sheets and the weight of the blankets above me. My face turned with a smile toward the glorious sun streaming in through the curtains I'd forgotten to close before going to bed.

Except…I hadn't gone to bed at all. We'd been trying to watch TV, then talking….

Before falling asleep in Jason's arms. Oh, man. Awkward City. All he wanted was to go to his room and get some sleep, and there I'd been, cozying up to him wearing nothing but a giant t-shirt. I never even made it under the covers before passing out. He must've put me to bed, tucked me in. I prayed my shirt had stayed in place. Flashing him on top of everything else would be too much. I'd have to resign my seat and join the Embarrassment Protection Program.

A glance around the room told me that, whatever happened, he wasn't still here. The mirrored closet doors showed the open bathroom, no lights. He wouldn't be in there. He must've gotten into his room after I passed out.

With a groan, I leaned back and rolled over, intending to

smother my mortification away with a pillow. Instead, my eyes landed on a note on the nightstand.

Lana –

I plugged your phone in for you. Text me when you wake up.

- J

My eyes shut as another wave of humiliation crashed over me. The last thing I wanted was to face Jason, but, well, he was my ride home. More importantly, he was my ride back to Governor Abbot, who I still needed to find and talk to before Monday morning. I didn't for a moment think we were lucky enough that she would have also taken shelter in this very hotel, especially because according to Curtis, her camper was more luxurious and snow-resistant than the entire building. Her satellite dish wouldn't dare go on the fritz, even in a blizzard. The governor had loved roughing it when she was younger, but now that she was pushing sixty, Curtis said she wanted to enjoy her time off to the fullest.

According to my good friend Abby, the diner next door typically opened for breakfast at six o'clock in the morning. It had to be long past that, even though I'd fallen asleep around eight last night. No wonder I felt so amazing. I couldn't remember the last time I'd slept ten hours in a row, but I strongly suspected it was when I got pneumonia my junior year of college.

Grabbing my phone, I checked the time and was surprised to find it was seven-fifteen. Jason was probably awake. We should get on the road as soon as possible. I needed breakfast first, though. Fast meant grabbing donuts or muffins at the gas station where he'd bought our t-shirts and toothbrushes the night before. However, if we were going to be hiking again, I could use a big breakfast—with some protein and maybe a fruit bowl.

Me: Hey. Are you awake?

Jason: Good morning, sunshine. How are you feeling?

Me: Like a million bucks. Slept like a baby. You?
Jason: Starved.
Me: What a coincidence. Want to meet at the diner at 7:30?

Not waiting for a reply, I hurried to the bathroom to brush my teeth and put on yesterday's clothes. Turning my panties inside-out wasn't ideal, but it beat going commando on a hiking expedition.

When I left my room, Jason was stepping out into the hall from his own doorway. I was worried things would be awkward after the night before, but he just said, "Hey, stranger," and fell into step beside me.

The diner was surprisingly crowded, but then again, the storm closed the highway and probably drove a lot of people to this hotel. Luckily, we got a table right away before my stomach started growling. Until we found Governor Abbot, I would be a stress ball. That didn't combine well with extreme hunger.

"While we're waiting for our food," Jason said after we put our menus away, "is there anything you'd like to talk about? Any questions you have about the Senate procedure or upcoming bills? Maybe, I don't know, if we're going to vote on something next week, this would be a good opportunity to bring it up now."

"Ouch."

"You deserved that."

"Ok, fine, I did," I said begrudgingly. "I accept responsibility for my actions. And we can talk about whatever you want on the drive back home later. But for now, I'd like to go over how we're going to find the campsite."

"You have a map, right? You never told me what happened yesterday."

"Steve happened. Jerk led us in a giant circle. He didn't want me to find the governor. Everything you said about him was right." Jason shook his head but said nothing. I jabbed a finger at him. "Go ahead. I know you're dying to say 'I told you so.'"

"Told you what? That Steve's a manipulative jerk? That's not a secret. He *is* a lobbyist."

"Another zinger. Are you always this punchy in the mornings?"

"No, not always. Only when my protégé ignores my advice, casts the deciding vote in a contentious and terrible law, then goes traipsing through the forest in a snowstorm and has to be rescued, stranding both of us at a hotel in the middle of nowhere overnight."

And the hits kept on coming. "Go on, go on. Say everything you're thinking. I deserve it."

He shook his head. "No, I'm done now. And I'm teasing. You made a mistake, okay. It happens to the best of us."

I faked a gasp as the waitress returned and put two plates in front of us. "You? Mr. Perfect? You've made mistakes? Say it ain't so!"

"Remind me to tell you about the time I made a typo in a child support bill that would have eliminated all past-due support."

I choked on my eggs. "You didn't."

He nodded sagely. "Luckily, someone caught it on the first reading. But imagine the disaster if it had passed."

The server returned to our table with Eggs Benedict and hash browns for me, pancakes, bacon, and eggs for Jason, and more importantly, two steaming, large mugs of coffee. Looking at everything brightened my mood considerably.

We chatted easily as we ate, then Jason called Governor Abbot's Chief of Staff to confirm whether she'd decided to cut her camping trip short or return to the woods. No point in going to find her if she was returning to her mansion. I knew exactly how to get there.

While I waited, I pulled out the video Ty made the day

before. The directions truly were fairly straightforward—the thing that got me lost was the liar I'd made the mistake of bringing with me. Jason and I should find the site fairly easily when no one was trying to sabotage us.

Putting away his phone, he nodded. "They left her RV last night, and she's already on her way back."

"She going to finish camping with snow still on the ground?"

"People do it all the time. She's hardcore. Besides, it's already almost fifty. Snow's melting." He signaled for the check. "You ready?"

My phone was fully charged. The video had been saved to my device along with a couple of Google maps. The downloaded files would work even if I lost the signal again. This time, we were fully prepared.

Snatching the bill out of his hand, I stood. "Let's go."

Without the snowstorm, it took less than an hour to get back to the woods. Funny how much faster you get somewhere when you're able to drive the speed limit. The first thing I noticed was that the parking lot Steve had told me to use wasn't the one Ty directed us to. I couldn't believe I hadn't seen it immediately. We'd been talking and laughing, and—it was all part of his distraction. My fingers dug into my palms. If only it was okay to strangle someone who deserved it.

I cursed under my breath.

"Language! That's five bucks in the swear jar," Jason said.

"I knew I shouldn't have told you about my swear jar," I grumbled. "Sometimes swearing is completely appropriate. And worth the money."

Another hundred yards down the path, we turned into the much larger lot I'd expected to find yesterday. A playground sat at the east end beside a large public restroom. This was the place. I knew it. I couldn't believe I'd followed Steve so innocently. If I hadn't called him out, we'd still be wandering around in circles a quarter mile away from where we were supposed to be, on the wrong side of the main road. That's what I got for trusting someone just because they spoke a good game and feigned interest in me.

With the help of my phone, I followed the path, which was much more of a walking trail than the one Steve and I had taken. No fallen logs to climb over. No steep tracks. In the wake of the storm, Jason and I had to carefully navigate some muddy areas, but the snow mostly melted by the time we got there. Welcome to New York. Blizzard one day, sixty degrees the next. Even in April.

It made more sense that this trail would lead to a campsite than the one I'd been wandering yesterday, especially considering the public restroom at the end of the trail (not to mention the showers).

We walked purposefully, being careful with the sights and signs, but not engaging in any unnecessary conversation that might take our attention off our goal. I was not going to get lost again. I was not going to get caught off guard. I was going to find Governor Abbot and convince her to veto the Schools Zoning and Protection Act or die trying. Preferably the first one.

Finally, about forty-five minutes after we left the car behind, I found what Ty had described as the final turn before the campsite. All we needed to do was locate an opening in the thick brush, push it aside, and come through the other side into the clearing. He said people used the unmarked trail as a shortcut all the time when they weren't carrying stuff.

"There!" Jason pointed at a spot in the hedge where several branches appeared to be broken off. Someone had tied a ratty old piece of cloth to one of the sturdier branches, so faded, it was impossible to tell what color it used to be.

"You think so? You want to push through a wall of bushes and hope we wind up where we're supposed to?" I didn't hear anything ahead, but maybe the governor and her family were napping or fishing. "This isn't the entrance to Narnia."

He grinned at me. "Sometimes you've got to have a little faith."

A little faith, indeed. Ty's directions had gotten us this far. No turning back now. With a deep breath, I burst through the brush into an open area, right where Ty said it would be. What I didn't expect was tripping over a tree root immediately beyond the hidden path. Stumbling, I pin-wheeled my arms to catch my balance. With effort, I managed to stay upright.

On the far side of the clearing sat an enormous RV, at least three times the size of Ty's. Also at least three decades newer. It gleamed in the sunlight, all sleek and black with tinted windows. The sides had been pulled out, which I knew from the tiny house shows I'd watched made the inside twice as big as a regular RV. I imagined the decor to be fabulous.

The vehicle sat about ten feet behind a fire pit, where a woman in a giant straw hat knelt on a piece of plywood, arranging dirt and leaves. I couldn't see her face, but the man sitting nearby in a camp chair strongly resembled the governor's husband Pete. Mr. Abbot rarely made public appearances, preferring to keep a low profile, but was easily recognizable because he strongly resembled Tom Hanks.

The brush crackled around me, coming alive. The air hummed. Suddenly, four men appeared. Stocky men with forearms the size of tree trunks, dressed the same in camouflage jackets and dark glasses. Each pointed a gun in my direction.

Fork me.

Chapter Seventeen

Jason was right. Coming here had been a terrible idea. I should have found any other way to get into contact with the governor. I should have stolen the approved bill off her desk and shredded it. Anything that wouldn't get me shot in the middle of the forest a hundred miles from home.

Not even daring to breathe, I raised my hands over my head one inch at a time. The brush rustled behind me, and two of the armed men moved their guns from me to point at the bushes. A muffled buzzing filled the air. It sounded like my ears were ringing but from somewhere else. A far-away radio? How near were other people?

"Don't shoot!" I raised my voice to the point of hysteria, both because *there were men pointing guns at me* and because I hoped Jason would hear me and run as fast as he could in the other direction. Looking past the guards, I started speaking quickly in hopes I could finish my sentence before someone shot me.

"Governor Abbot, my name is Lana Chen. Tiberius Baker told me where to find you. Curtis is a friend of mine. I know this is highly inappropriate, and I just realized that you're probably going to have me arrested, but we need to talk about the Schools Zoning and Protection Act."

The entire time I spoke, Governor Abbot continued working in the fire pit, not even glancing up. Whatever she was doing must require high levels of concentration. Her husband, on the other hand, never took his eyes off me.

Jason emerged from the bushes beside me, hands up. "Hey, Pete. How's it going?"

"Oh, man, do they just let anyone in here these days?" The smile on Mr. Abbot's face as he rose showed he was joking. As he walked toward us, he bent down and touched Governor Abbot on the shoulder.

She leaned back on her heels and sat up, taking in the scene before her. A look of surprise crossed her face as if she noticed the two of us for the first time. I'd never seen someone so focused on loading up a fire pit, but then again, I'd never built a fire. A skill that, come to think of it, I should probably develop in case I ever decide to go on a trek through the forest in the dead of winter to track down a public official and get ditched by the guy I'm dating who turned out to just be using me for votes.

Huh. Suddenly I wondered if Jason knew how to build a fire. Just in case.

Governor Abbot removed a pair of wireless earbuds, and suddenly things made a lot more sense. She hadn't realized we were there. That also explained the noises I'd been hearing: those babies were turned up L-O-U-D.

"Hello. What are you doing here?"

Jason spoke first, slowly, and projecting his voice. At the same time, he moved his hands. "Governor Abbot, we're sorry to barge in on you like this, but I promise, it's for a good cause. I beg you, please give us a moment of your time."

She tapped one ear, then turned toward the trailer. "I'll be right back."

My gaze went back and forth between Jason and the governor. "Where is she going?"

His face turned red, and he stuttered. My eyes went to his hands, and I slowly realized that he hadn't been gesturing.

"She can't wear hearing aids with her earbuds, but Chris loves having the newest tech." Mr. Abbott said. First man Abbott? I wasn't sure what the right form of address was.

Finally, I got it. "She's Deaf."

"My wife is Hard of Hearing," he said. "We mostly don't share that with strangers, but if you're with this guy, you might be okay."

For the first time, I realized that I'd never seen a public or official image of Governor Abbot with her hair swept back from her face. It was always down, arranged over her ears.

"Ah, thank you for trusting me. Your secret is safe with me."

"Don't make me regret it," he said. "I'd offer you a drink, but, well, I don't want you to think you're welcome to stay."

After all of Steve's smooth-talking and lies, Mr. Abbott's gruff honesty felt refreshing. Marching over, I offered my hand. "Pete, right? It's a pleasure to meet you."

"Under any other circumstances, I would say the same." He glanced at his watch. "Once Chris gets back, you have five minutes before I tell our guards to toss you out on your butts."

"Deal," I said. "Thank you for not doing that already."

His lips twitched. "I still might, seeing you brought this guy."

"Look, Pete, at some point you're going to have to get over me beating you at basketball. Every time we play."

"Listen up, big man, I'll give you a rematch any time."

"You're just saying that because there's no hoop around for miles."

Despite their faux-hostile banter, it was clear these two had known each other for a long time. They shared an easy rapport that only came with familiarity. Before I could ask them about it, Governor Abbot returned. Now that I looked at her ears, I saw her hearing aids clearly.

"You have ten minutes to tell me what you're doing here," she said without preamble.

"That's very generous of you, ma'am," I said. "Your husband only gave me five."

Her expression was inscrutable. "And you've just wasted the first twelve seconds."

Without further prompting, I launched into the speech I'd been preparing ever since I got the hare-brained idea to drive up here in the first place. I somehow sensed she might not be sympathetic to Steve's role in the whole thing, so I downplayed it. Strong women often didn't appreciate other women blaming men for their problems, and to be honest, he didn't make me do anything. I was my own person who sometimes made bad choices.

Nothing on the governor's face gave me the slightest inkling what she was thinking, so I laid it all on the line. She stopped me twice, asking me to repeat things or slow down. When I finished, three of my ten minutes remained. Not bad.

"Let me get this straight," she said when I finished, hands on her hips. "You voted in favor of a bill without reading it. The bill passed by one vote—yours. You found out after the fact that, if you had read it, you would have voted against it. And now you want me to exercise my veto power because you failed to do your job properly?"

When she put it like that, I sounded horribly incompetent. My cheeks burned. "I made a mistake, Governor. I'm here to fix it."

She sighed. "To make matters worse, you somehow found my private vacation getaway—which I have been using for decades and will now have to change. You crashed my alone time, of which there isn't much these days. To do a favor for you, a junior Senator I have never met who has been in the job all of two weeks?"

I swallowed. "Yes, ma'am."

"Go. Get out of here before I have my guards remove you. This is unbelievably inappropriate behavior. And Jason? You know better."

He looked as ashamed as I felt. "Yes, Governor. I'm sorry."

"Me, too. So sorry," I said.

She waved her hands. "Don't apologize. Leave."

Without another word, I hung my head and headed back for the path. She was right, of course. Everything she said was right. I'd made a huge mistake. Then, in trying to fix it, I'd made everything worse by asking Ty to betray a confidence. Steve and Jason now both knew where the governor's private vacation getaway was. I didn't worry about Jason, but what might Steve do with that information? He'd clearly established that he couldn't be trusted. That he would exploit every possible opportunity to get what he wanted. The only silver lining was that I couldn't conceive of any possible way he'd ever actually find his way here, much less be able to direct someone else.

A tear dripped down my cheek, plopping into the dust at my feet. I needed to get to the next clearing over before I lost it. On top of everything else, I couldn't let Governor Abbot and her armed guards see me cry.

Jason leaned over wordlessly and took my hand as we made our way through the bushes. A small gesture, but it made me feel a tiny bit better. This trip had been a complete disaster, a terrible idea from start to finish, but at least I was finding out who my real friends were.

I glanced to my left. "Thanks for coming with me. I'm sorry that I'm such a hot mess."

"Come on. This is way more fun than listening to Rumsfeld

bloviate about windmills or reducing the death tax in committee meetings all morning."

I chuckled, and a tiny thrill hit me at the twinkle in his eyes. A shiver went down my spine, beginning where our fingers were still linked.

"True, true," I said. "But seriously. I appreciate it. I appreciate *you*."

He squeezed my hand. "I'm just glad I could be here for you."

"There's no one I would rather wander lost in the woods with."

"That's what friends are for, right?"

"Right." But even as I agreed, I wondered: were we friends? My mind went back to last night in the motel. The thoughtful way he'd picked out a toothbrush and t-shirt for me to sleep in (despite the fact that I missed his text).

The way it felt to fall asleep in Jason's arms.

Chapter Eighteen

My spirits sank considerably as we continued our trek out of the forest. The more time I spent with my thoughts, the more I realized I'd screwed over thousands of people and there was nothing I could do about it. Governor Abbot didn't even want to hear my explanation. Coming out here had been a terrible idea, and I didn't have any better ones.

The bill had passed. I could help Mel mount a constitutional challenge—and I would, but those took time. That also assumed my best friend was still willing to speak to me once she found out what I did. As soon as Jason got me back to civilization, I needed to drive over to the site of the new Push and Pole Fitness and face the music (once I fixed my stupid flat tire, which I now strongly suspected Steve had done while I was inside changing). I dreaded the conversation with every fiber of my being.

At the same time, I deserved whatever I got. Trudging through the forest with mud clinging to my shoes while the sun dehydrated my skin was a small price to pay for putting my best friend out of business. So was losing the entire investment

I put into Push and Pole, because if Governor Abbot signed the bill, we wouldn't be able to operate. We'd put the deposit down on the studio. Mel had found a contractor to start work on repairing the floor right away. At the time, I'd been grateful, but now I'd like to have my money back. Not to mention the poles we'd ordered, which had been delivered yesterday. The landlord couldn't find another pole fitness studio to move in if the law stopped us from operating. Mel and I didn't have the knowledge or experience to use the space for anything else.

What would we do? Teach pole climbing? Pole vault? Fireman training? Jousting?

With these thoughts consuming me, it felt like far less time to find our way back to the car than to get to the Governor's campsite. Thank goodness for small favors. As soon as my feet hit the pavement, they stopped moving. This whole time, I'd been fueled by the mission, then by the need to not get stuck overnight in the middle of nowhere again.

Now? There was nothing to keep me going. I dropped to the pavement and lowered my head into my hands. Where had things gone so wrong? My whole life, I'd done whatever was expected of me. Good grades, college, law school. Got a well-paying, if not exciting, job. Then an exciting job my best friend got for me because I lacked any motivation of my own. A job I completely ruined in under two weeks, destroying my best friend's career in the process.

Maybe if I closed my eyes and wished real hard, when I woke up, I'd discover I'd decided to follow in Dad's footsteps and become a pilot rather than getting a law degree. Then I could fly far, far away from here and avoid the entire nightmare of my life.

"Lana?" Jason's voice sounded far away. Peeking through my fingers, I discovered he'd made it almost halfway across the parking lot before realizing I wasn't with him. "Are you okay?"

Not trusting myself to speak, I simply shook my head. I was

most certainly not okay. I'd ruined everything, and I didn't have any idea how to fix it.

A moment later, a pair of hiking boots entered the tiny circle of my vision. "Shh. We can get through this. There has to be a solution."

Instead of replying, a massive sob escaped me. I couldn't speak. I couldn't breathe. Part of me expected him to turn and run back to the car. I wouldn't blame Jason if he started avoiding me. But instead, he settled onto the pavement beside me. He didn't tell me to shush, didn't try to comfort me. He let me cry.

I didn't know how much time passed before I got control of myself. Finally, I took a deep breath, wiped my eyes, and blew my nose on a tissue from my pocket. "Thank you. I'm so sorry."

"Nothing to apologize for," he said. "I'm here for you."

Looking up, I saw the same tenderness in his eyes I'd noticed last night. They were an absolutely gorgeous shade of amber. Holding him like this felt right.

All I needed to do was tilt my head back a little, lean into him, and press my lips against his. Take the comfort he offered.

And yet…it was all wrong. I'd started spending time with Steve because he was the first person at the legislature to make an effort to get to know me. Would I have liked him if I'd met him after making other friends? I'd never know. Now that he'd turned out to be a jerk, Jason was here, convenient. I needed to stop grabbing onto anything—or anyone—that came along. It didn't matter that Jason was smart and gorgeous and sexy and caring and kind. Not when I was such an incredible mess.

I stepped back, avoiding his eyes and the feeling of disappointment settling into my belly. "I'm sorry for everything. Let's go home."

"Right." My mind wanted to believe he sounded disappointed, but I wasn't ready to trust my instincts. They'd failed me one time too many recently. "Let's go home."

We walked across the parking lot in silence, our earlier companionable distance stretching into a chasm. Finally, I couldn't take the quiet any longer. "You never told me you know ASL."

"You never asked."

"Touché."

"I took it in high school. Kept it up because it helps me serve all of my constituents better." After a moment, he said, "What languages do you speak?"

"English, French, German, and Japanese," I said.

"Japanese? I thought you were Chinese."

"Chinese-American," I said. "My grandparents moved to New York before my mother was born. They wanted her to fit in, so they only taught her English. Mom's parents never spoke Cantonese at home. Dad learned it as a kid but never taught me. I picked up Japanese when he was stationed in Japan."

"That's impressive."

I shrugged. "Some people are good at sports or drawing or math. I'm good with languages. I like the way knowing the native tongue helped me connect with people, especially because we moved around so much."

"Every time I think I'm getting to know the real Lana, I discover I've barely scratched the surface."

"Well, stick around. In time, you'll learn more."

"I can't wait."

A loud rumble filled the air.

With horror, I realized the sound came from my stomach. "I know we have to get back to work, and we've been gone way too long already, but would you mind stopping to pick up lunch? A drive-thru is fine."

He pushed the starter button and leaned forward. "Not a problem, because we need gas. The sooner, the better. I was in a hurry to get back to you at the hotel, so I didn't fill up last night. I forgot this morning."

Ten miles down the road, he pulled over at a small gas station attached to a sandwich shop. Cheap, not-too-greasy, and fast, just the way I liked it. Jason pulled in at the pump, and I went in to place our order while he filled the tank.

The sandwich shop was small but clean. They offered essentially the same varieties you could find at any one of hundreds of similar locations throughout the country. I found the familiarity comforting. It was early enough that there weren't any other customers, but a cashier waited behind the counter, tapping away on her phone. She looked about nineteen, with blond hair pulled back into a messy ponytail, a smattering of freckles across her snub nose, and a name tag identifying her as Robyn.

When she looked up and saw me standing there, her eyes widened. "Hey! It's you! You're the senator/stripper lady."

Not exactly, but whatever. I wasn't in the mood to start a debate. "I'm Senator Lana Chen."

"That's so cool!"

"To be honest, I'm surprised you've heard of me this far north."

"Oh, everyone knows who you are." She peered out the window. "Hold up. Is that the other guy?"

My gaze followed her pointing finger, although it seemed obvious who I would find. "That's Senator Park. He's a representative from the Bronx."

She squealed and clapped. "This is so awesome! OMG, I can't believe you're here."

"Thanks," I said cautiously. *Please don't let her ask me to autograph something.*

Robyn's enthusiasm seemed a bit excessive, and I was starving, so I turned my attention to the menu board behind her head. She went back to her phone. After a moment, I relayed our order and handed over my credit card. She seemed way too jazzed about making sandwiches, but maybe it was a slow morning. The weather wouldn't warm up for a few more weeks, and this wasn't the best skiing area, so they might not see a lot of traffic these days.

"For here, right?" Robin asked as she handed me a bag with two sandwiches and two bottles of water.

I shook my head. "No, we need to get back on the road. To go."

Not to mention, this entire place was starting to give me the heebie-jeebies. My parents' German Shepherd hadn't been this excited to see me last time I went home for dinner.

"Come on! You've got to stay. You just got here."

"I appreciate that, but it's not an option," I said, "I'm sorry."

She huffed, but once I held out my hand, she begrudgingly put our sandwiches in a bag and handed it over. For a minute, I'd been afraid she was going to hold them hostage until I promised to stay.

The bell over the door behind me jingled, and she clapped again. "It's him! It's really him!"

I resisted the urge to ask if she'd thought I was lying.

Never flustered, Jason walked up to the counter and put out his hand seamlessly. "Jason Park. Nice to meet you. And you are?"

"So stoked! You guys are going to put this place on the map."

"Excellent. Glad to hear it." He stepped toward me and turned, lowering his voice. "What's going on?"

"No idea," I said. "Some kind of hidden camera thing?"

"Maybe she's a fan?"

"Of me?" I snorted. "I don't have fans."

"You've got me. I happen to be very fond of you." His mouth was only inches from my ear. I could feel the heat of his breath against my cheek. Our eyes locked, and his pupils dilated. For a moment, I wondered if he was going to kiss me. I couldn't move. I couldn't breathe. It was too soon, so quickly after Steve's betrayal.

It didn't matter that I met Jason first, or that I'd liked him until Steve distracted me. Not at the moment. And not when Jason was my only real ally at the Senate right now. Never in my life had I moved easily from one guy to the next.

But Steve was a predator, someone who wormed his way in, telling me what he thought I wanted to hear. My feelings for him evaporated the moment he showed his true colors. If Steve was Fool's Gold, Jason was a diamond.

My tongue darted out to wet my lips. Jason's eyes followed the movement. What was he thinking? Did he know I wanted him to kiss me? Should I show him?

"Look, you guys gotta stay," Robyn said, interrupting the moment. I didn't know where to feel frustrated or relieved. "I texted all my friends."

I pressed my lips together while I searched for the right response. "Are your friends interested in state government?"

She snorted. "Of course not. But we love a good scandal!"

I chuckled. "Well, I'm sorry to tell you, I'm pretty boring. All the scandal happened before I got elected."

"Nu-uh," she said. "This is great stuff."

Beside me, the color drained from Jason's face. It was starting to feel like the two of them were acting out a scene from a play, and the director had forgotten to give me a copy of the script. Hands on my hips, I said, "Wait. What's going on?"

"You don't know?" Robyn asked. "Haven't you seen the news?"

"I'm afraid not. We've been traveling all day."

"Right." She nodded. "We sell the local paper in the gas station next door. You should check it out."

Without responding, I fled through the archway leading to the adjacent convenience shop. By the front counter, I found newspapers for Albany, Saratoga County, and nearby Lake George. The same picture graced the front of all three. With a gasp, I skidded to a halt. My hands went up to cover my mouth. I couldn't breathe. Now I knew how Mel felt when a reporter found her doing street pole and plastered it across the front page.

At least street pole was cool, though. This? Not cool.

"A SENATE AFFAIR," Jason read from the front page. "Long-Time New York Senator Spends Night with Recently Elected Stripper."

"What is even happening right now?" As usual, I ignored the stripper comment. Disputing it here and now wouldn't get it removed from the paper. That also didn't seem to be the worst part of the headline, not by a long shot.

His eyes scanned the page before he answered. "Someone from the media spotted us entering the hotel last night and noticed that we never left. They appeared to miss the foot of snow on the ground."

"That's ridiculous! We slept in separate rooms. Nothing happened. What were we supposed to do, strap on a snowplow?"

Grabbing the paper from his hand, I stared at the words as if they would make more sense this way. But no, there we were, standing in the hotel lobby last night as snow fell. The caption proudly announced we had checked in to a single room the night before. Seriously, who knew we were here? And why did anyone care? Also, no one bothered to find out Jason got a separate room later? What shoddy reporting.

Something else tugged at the back of my mind, but I couldn't quite grasp it. Jason held out his hand, so I gave the paper back, wanting the thing out of my sight ASAP.

"I know, I know. But you know as well as anyone that appearance often substitutes for reality."

"Oh, well. At least I don't care what they think of me." Something about the headline made me stop. Affair, affair. What? Then I read the subheading: *Senator Park spent the evening with a lovely lady, not his wife.*

"Whoa, whoa, whoa. You're still *married?*"

The color drained from Jason's face as I watched, giving me my answer. I couldn't believe it. Married. He was still married. Or remarried. Maybe he was already on Wife #2. Either way, he'd lied to me.

Just when I thought we'd been getting close to something. So stupid! We'd been growing closer, and he flirted with me, like I flirted with him… My eyes darted to his left hand, no ring.

So not entirely my fault, then. Apparently, I needed to ask. They always said, when you assume, you make a butt out of "u and me." Okay, that's not how they said it, but I was determined to stick to my no swearing, even when my world was collapsing at my feet.

"Married," I repeated. "And you said I'm full of surprises. I thought you were divorced."

"I am! There has to be a mistake."

"Like, you accidentally got a marriage license and said 'I do'? How does that happen?"

"Don't be like that."

"Like what? Tell me how I should be, Jason. If that is your real name."

He didn't know my feelings for him were changing. Maybe the past twenty hours or so hadn't affected him the way I'd thought. Heck, even I didn't understand how I felt. He was my mentor. My friend. Or so I'd thought. Friends didn't lie about who they were.

"Of course it's my real name. I can explain. I just…"

"Sorry, I've got to go." Before he could respond, I bolted for the ladies' room and locked myself inside. I refused to leave until he did. Sure, I didn't have a car, but I could call a Lyft. This didn't seem like the best time to count on Mel to come get me.

Robyn would probably be delighted to give me a ride home, but an hour in a car with her wasn't going to solve any of my problems.

"Lana!" Jason's voice echoed behind me, but I didn't stop. It didn't matter.

How dare he warn me away from Steve, act jealous, when he was married to someone else? How dare he be so kind and sweet and considerate! Or act like he'd wanted to kiss me back there? Okay, fine, nothing had happened, but the way he treated me so often hinted he would be open to more. I couldn't shake the idea that something might have happened if I hadn't started dating Steve.

"Something" apparently meant the breaking of vows. That's why he'd been helping me. Just like Steve, all Jason wanted was to charm me and find out what it was like to sleep with a stripper. They were two peas in a pod. I was a fool for trusting either of them.

Ten minutes later, my car arrived. I walked straight toward it without turning my head to the left or right. If Jason was still around, I didn't want to see him.

Halfway home, I made a split decision not to head to my place. He knew where I lived, and if he decided to drop by to talk to me, I didn't want to see him. My phone had been buzzing non-stop, so I'd finally muted him. The temptation to hit "block" was strong, but we still had to work together. I couldn't avoid him forever.

I could, however, avoid him for the rest of the day. After offering my driver an additional ten-dollar tip, he changed course and took me to the site of what would eventually become Push and Pole Fitness. I'd get Mel to take my home later.

The studio wasn't open for business yet, since we had only signed the lease a week and a half ago. A good thing, because it meant there would be no witnesses to my confession. I couldn't believe the difference Mel had made already. The remainder of the old, moldy floors had been ripped out, replaced with gleaming, hardwood. She'd buffed everything by hand while waiting for the new poles to arrive. The windows and mirrors shone, and the lighting fixtures we'd picked out online illuminated every inch of the space, making it bright and inviting.

Mel sat inside at the front desk when I arrived. She hadn't fully set up everything, but we had a computer and printer and tablet for processing credit card payments. I'd been excited last week when we found everything on clearance, but now the sight of the electronics made my heart sink. Items bought on final sale couldn't be returned.

One look at my tear-streaked face brought my best friend to my side. "What happened?"

I told her everything, not bothering to sugarcoat my own failures. She deserved to know the entire ugly truth. Her face grew whiter and whiter as I spoke, but she didn't say a word until I moaned out an apology at the end.

To my surprise, when I finished, she hugged me. "Don't worry. It'll be okay."

"How?"

"Well, I'm not sure at the moment, but we'll figure something out. I'll call Daniel. He'll help."

"Maybe I should quit and dump all my problems in my best friend's lap." A wry smile accompanied my words, but even giving voice to them showed how down I felt. Luckily, Mel knew me well enough not to take offense.

She laughed. "Ouch. Okay, I deserved that."

I sighed. "No, you didn't. I'm the one who accepted the job. I was excited about it. I voted for a bad bill. I decided to stay in Saratoga last night. I, apparently, spent the night with a married man."

"Oh, Lana," she said. "Did you—?"

"No! Nothing happened. But even if it had, I didn't know he was married." I sank down into the chair she'd vacated and buried my head in my hands. "What am I going to do?"

Chapter Nineteen

It didn't seem right for Mel to comfort me for ruining her, even if the collateral damage would hit me, too. After I got myself back together, apologized forty-seven more times, and promised to make it right, I told her I'd get a Lyft instead of asking her for a ride. Since I was *going* to make this right, she needed to be ready to open on time.

Halfway home, like a bolt of lightning, the answer hit me. I knew what I needed to do. This all started when Mel's video went viral and people freaked out about pole fitness in their area.

Time to make a video my own.

Twenty minutes later, I stood in the middle of my living room, now wearing jade green, four-inch high platform heels, matching booty shorts covered in glitter, and a white sports bra. My hair was in a ponytail, my face clean and free of makeup. No pretense, just me and the pole.

With a deep breath, I hit the record button and stepped back. "Hi. My name is Lana Chen, and I'm the New York State Senator for the district of Saratoga Springs. I got this job by accident, from the write-in vote. It all started when my best friend Mel made a video that went viral. She fell off the pole when her ex-boyfriend burst in with another woman. You may have seen it. If that hadn't happened, if he hadn't been using her place the way he used her during her relationship, a couple dozen people would have seen the video. Unfortunately, it spread like wildfire and set off a backlash of politicians who wanted to shut down pole fitness for good. Mel fought back, running for office to stop them. Ultimately, I got voted into her spot—and I'm grateful for that—but still, people are trying to stop us from dancing.

"I made a huge mistake. I admit that. Last week I voted for a bill that, unknown to me, included a clause that, once again, would stop women like my friend Mel from using pole dancing or pole fitness to make a living. When I realized my mistake, I went to the governor and asked her to help me, but she refused. Now I'm asking you, the people of New York, to help me make this right. Share this video. Watch it, retweet it, post it on your own pages. Tell your stories. Show Governor Abbot how signing this bill would put New Yorkers at risk."

I turned and walked toward the pole. "Pole is many things. To me, it's about strength. Inner and outer strength. Inner strength because of the haters. Outer strength required for these types of moves." I placed my left palm against the pole near the bottom, then reached over my head and grasped the top with my right hand. Slowly, inch by inch, I moved my body into an X position, holding it there. "Pole is about knowing your body, about trusting it. And about not letting other people get to you."

Instead of lowering myself to the ground, I swirled around the pole into a sitting position. "Here's the move Mel was performing when she got interrupted. It's not easy."

My legs split, and the ground rushed toward me, just the way it had with Mel in her fateful video. Near the bottom, I snapped my legs together, halting my descent, and leaving me curled around the pole. I waited for a beat before standing and taking a bow. "Mel taught me that move. She taught me a lot of things, including how to be strong and stand up for myself. How to stand up for all of you."

After stopping the video, I rewatched it. Not perfect, but good enough. This wasn't about being perfect. It was about being me. Then I played again, making a full transcript to include at the top. Finally, I navigated to my official Facebook page, which Linda usually maintained for me. I typed my plea for help at the top, pasted in the transcript so Governor Abbot could read it easily, crossed my fingers and toes, and hit "post." It only took a second to share to Twitter and Instagram.

Then I waited.

Less than two minutes later, my phone beeped with a text.

Jason: Nice video. I'm proud of you for not giving up.

Jason: Look, I know you're upset. But if you'll give me five minutes, I can explain everything.

It took everything in me not to respond. But now wasn't the time. I wasn't in the right headspace to worry about my love life.

Once the video was posted for the world to see, I was too nervous to sit online and watch the responses come in. I was already dressed for a workout, so I decided to pump up the music and release some nervous energy.

I was finishing up when someone knocked at my front door. I jumped at the interruption before glancing at the clock on my Blu-Ray player. Who would come to my house at nine-thirty in the evening?

It was a short list, and I didn't want to see two-thirds of the people on it. Jason didn't know I was developing feelings for him, couldn't know how much it hurt to find out he was married, and I wasn't in the mood to tell him. Also, he wouldn't show up after I ignored his texts.

Halfway to the door, I realized I was still wearing my

workout clothes: a sports bra and booty shorts. Oh, well. Someone was about to get an eyeful. Not that it mattered. The whole world could see it now.

Through the peephole, I saw a hand with perfectly manicured nails smoothing down a baseball cap. Not Mel, then. Teaching pole with long nails got hazardous.

The door swung open, and my eyes widened. "Governor Abbot?"

"Good evening, Senator Chen." A feather could have knocked me over. Without waiting for my response, she pushed the door open and walked past. "You don't mind if I come in, do you? I'd rather not be seen on your doorstep."

When the door shut behind her, I finally snapped out of my stupor. "Yes, of course. I'm sorry. Please, come in. Sorry for my appearance."

She turned around to face me and tapped her ear. "What? Louder, please."

Oops. I'd remembered the aids, but my voice barely came out as a whisper.

"Sorry!" I repeated my invitation, this time speaking from the diaphragm.

"Don't be silly. You can wear whatever you want in your own home."

"Thank you, but let me throw on a sweatshirt. Please have a seat." I led her to the couch, then started to hurry off down the hall before turning back. "Would you like something to drink? Coffee? Tea?"

"Do you have wine?" At my startled look, she laughed. "We're not on the clock, Senator Chen. My husband is waiting in the car around the corner. He'll pick me up when we're done."

What in the world was happening? The governor of the state of New York was sitting on my couch asking for a glass of wine while I stood half-naked in front of her, too stunned to form coherent sentences.

One thing at a time. I raced to my bedroom, grabbed a hoodie, and yanked an over-sized pair of yoga pants over my shorts. Not exactly fit for an audience with the top official in the state, but a huge improvement. Besides, as Governor Abbot pointed out, she was the one who dropped by unannounced.

Back in the kitchen, I grabbed a bottle of wine off the counter, along with two glasses. Then I stopped and opened the bottle before re-entering the living room. She probably didn't care I bought twist-off instead of corked bottles, but what if she was a wine snob? I didn't even own a corkscrew, not since Mel and I discovered the same wine goes into corked and uncorked bottles. They just charge more for one.

I filled each glass generously before taking a deep breath and walking back through the doorway. I didn't know if she read lips, so I did my best to speak clearly. "I hope you like Merlot. It's all I have."

"Merlot is lovely, thank you." She took the glass and inhaled the liquid before taking a tentative sip. A ghost of a smile crossed her lips. She took a larger mouthful and savored it for a moment before swallowing. "What a gorgeous bouquet. Is this local?"

My face grew warm. "No, actually. I am a big fan of New York wines, but this is from California. A small winery my best friend and I visited a few years ago. Every Christmas, we split a case."

"What a lovely tradition," she said. "This friend—are you talking about Melody Martin, the pole fitness instructor?"

"Yes, ma'am. Mel."

"Oh, dear, please don't ma'am me. Not when I'm sitting on your couch having a drink late at night. I'm here to chat."

"Yes, ma'am. Sorry. I mean…What can I do for you, Governor Abbot?"

Her voice grew stern. "First of all, I don't need to tell you how inappropriate it was for you to follow me into the woods."

"No. I am well aware. I didn't think I had any other choice. But I do apologize."

"Relax. I'm not here to lecture you. I'm not going to press charges or alert the press or anything. What I wanted to say is, that took guts. Then I saw your video—wow. You blew me away."

Wine caught in my throat. I must have misheard her, but all of a sudden, I couldn't breathe. With great effort, I managed to swallow. "I'm sorry, could you repeat that?"

"Certainly. That took guts. All of it. Admitting you made a mistake. Tracking me down. Jason told me you started your journey the day before, and not even a blizzard stopped your mission. Not to mention asking for a favor with six guns pointed at you." She set her now-empty glass on the table. "You remind me a lot of myself at your age. It's important for us marginalized women to stick together."

I thought for a moment, trying to remember her history. "When you were my age, you'd served on the city council and were preparing to run for your first Assembly term, right?"

"I see you've done your research."

My head dropped. "Not well enough. If I had, I would have voted against the Schools Zoning and Protection Act, and we wouldn't be sitting here."

"Fair enough." She started to say something else, then stopped and went into the kitchen. She returned with the bottle, which she used to top off both our glasses. "Why don't you tell me what happened?"

Oh, man. I desperately did not want to tell her how I'd stupidly let a smooth talker get the better of me. That was a secret I'd prefer to carry to my grave. Lana Chen was supposed to be smart. A hard worker. A person who did her homework. The woman who consulted Google roughly fourteen times a day and always had a lawyer joke handy. I couldn't admit I'd let a lobbyist trick me out of doing my research for the first time in my entire life.

And yet—for some reason, the governor had come to my condo at almost ten o'clock on a work night, the last night of her vacation. She obviously had something on her mind, and if I wanted to know what it was, I needed to play by her rules.

I went with the abbreviated version. "Someone intercepted the message about the vote being moved. I'm not sure how, but I didn't know we were voting. I thought I had until Monday to review everything."

"Jason told me about that, too. It sounds like you're filtering." She clucked her tongue and shook her head. "I've been in this business longer than you've been alive, and somehow I'm always still shocked at the ways men will take advantage of women. Steve knew he couldn't talk you into voting against the bill, so he tricked you."

"Exactly." I sighed. "I feel so stupid. None of this should have happened. But the bottom line, Governor, is that the bill is bad. It wasn't always bad. The earlier versions are fine. I read those. Nothing exciting, but nothing terrible, either. The originally proposed law closed a couple of loopholes. Made it more clear where certain types of businesses could be located."

"So what happened?"

"After the bill went through Appropriations, Rumsfeld requested another edit. That should have sent it back through the committees, but somehow it got passed through without a careful reading. I don't know if he lied about what the amendments were or if the members simply didn't care. Either way, the new bill stifles free expression. It'll close dance studios and yoga studios and pole fitness studios—and yes, strip clubs—adjacent to dual-zoned areas. It stops certain types of businesses from operating near schools, but it increases the radius and redefines schools so broadly that almost any place children might be qualifies." I took a deep breath. "Governor, if you sign this bill, it's going to put my best friend out of business. I can't be the reason she loses her job, that her dreams get taken away. But it's not only about her. This is going to affect a lot of people."

"No, it won't," she said gently. "I've read the amended bill."

My ears perked up. "You're going to veto?"

"No."

I shook my head. "I don't get it."

When the legislature was out of session, the governor could refuse to sign or veto a bill, and it would turn into what they called a "pocket veto." Essentially, the governor's inaction would stop the bill from passing if we weren't in session. But the legislature wouldn't be taking a recess for weeks. If Governor Abbot didn't sign or veto the bill within ten days, it would automatically become law.

"According to my assistant, the bill landed on my desk on Friday morning," she said. "Tomorrow is Monday. That means I have to make a decision by next Tuesday. You have a little over a week to convince your colleagues to pass a new, similar bill without the amendments. Get support to fix the regulations the bill was intended to fix, while also protecting freedom of expression."

"I don't understand," I said. "We don't have the votes to override a veto."

"You don't need to override. Fix it. If you draft a new bill, get the votes, and send it to my desk in time, I'll sign it and veto the Schools Zoning and Protection Act."

With every word she spoke, a weight lifted off my chest. I felt a thousand pounds lighter. For a split second, I wondered how she would react if I launched myself out of my seat and hugged her. Only the vision of National Guardsman swarming my living room stopped me. Instead, I squealed with delight. "This is unbelievable! Thank you. Thank you so much!"

"Don't thank me." She picked up her phone and started tapping out a text. "You got me thinking. You've got a lot of fire, Senator Chen. I admire that."

If Steve was right, everyone in the Senate thought I was a joke. Elected on a technicality. This was my one chance to show them they'd underestimated me. I had a law degree from Yale, graduated at the top of my class, was named a member of the Honor Society and recipient of the Outstanding Graduating Senior Award. I worked harder than anyone I knew. Yes, I'd made a mistake, but I was going to fix it. Last week hadn't been a total disaster after all.

I started to thank her again, but since she'd repeatedly told me not to, instead I held out my hand for a shake.

"Firm grip," she said. "I like that."

"Pole will do that for you," I said. "Let me know if you ever want a free lesson. I've got contacts."

Governor Abbot smiled. "Wouldn't that be something? Thank you for the drink, Senator Chen. Have your assistant call my assistant tomorrow to schedule a meeting for next Tuesday. See if Senator Park will join us."

I gulped at the mention, but absolutely nothing was going to ruin this chance for me. Especially not a misunderstanding with my greatest ally in the chamber. We needed to move past this. He didn't know I liked him. Maybe it was nothing—just the stress of the situation making everything seem sexy and charged with emotion. I'd obviously been watching too many Hallmark movies. "Absolutely. I'll talk to him first thing tomorrow morning."

"Excellent. I'll be going, then." She paused at the threshold and turned her head to look at me in her peripheral vision. "I'm putting a lot of faith in you, Lana. Don't let me down."

"I won't, Governor," I promised.

More importantly, I wouldn't let myself down. I would save Push and Pole Fitness if it was the last thing I did. I owed Mel, but besides that, I owed it to myself to see what I could do when I put my mind to it. No more coasting along, hoping to blend in, trying not to create any waves.

It was time for Lana Chen to make a splash.

Chapter Twenty

As soon as Governor Abbot drove away, I tossed the rest of my wine down the sink and put on a pot of coffee. No time to waste. New York had sixty-three senators, including me. For this to work, I needed to draft a new bill that kept the good provisions from the original and cut the bad. But then I also need to convince people to vote for the new law, which I'd titled the Miller Act after Mel.

Bringing everyone on board was no small task, considering that if everyone did nothing, we would wind up with the law we already passed. I had to convince people not only that the original law was bad, but that my proposed solution was better. Then it needed to pass the House, which passed the SZPA by a landslide and might not appreciate my changes.

A tall order, to say the least.

Knowing Governor Abbot would sign the Schools Zoning and Protection Act into law if nothing happened would make it tough to convince anyone to work with me. Especially since, as Steve so eloquently pointed out, most of the other legislators thought I was a joke. The Assembly had one hundred fifty seats, but if I could get the Senate on board, there was a good chance the Assembly would pass it. The Assembly Majority Leader was a friend of Jason's, and he had a long history of working with other people in both parties to pass important legislation.

I needed to convince Senate Majority Leader Diaz that protecting First Amendment rights was every bit as important as protecting property values from decline. My saving grace may be that the leader also came from New York City, where property values skyrocketed more every day and people were used to businesses intermingling with residences. She'd voted against the SZPA.

My first instinct was to call Jason and tell him what happened. I was already reaching for the phone when I realized it was almost eleven o'clock on a Sunday. His secret wife wouldn't appreciate him getting a call from some random woman practically in the middle of the night, especially after we spent the night at a hotel together (albeit unintentionally).

Instead, after a moment's thought, I sent a text to my favorite night owl.

Me: Hey, are you still up? I need to talk to you and Daniel.

Mel: You're in luck. We just finished a movie. Hold on.

A moment later, my tablet rang. Their faces filled the screen. By the time I finished telling them about Governor Abbot's visit, Daniel looked gobsmacked.

"Are you serious right now? This isn't a joke," Mel said.

I shook my head. "I can't believe it myself. But I've only got a week to change everyone's minds, my mentor and I aren't speaking because he lied to me, a lobbyist almost seduced me into distraction, and the only thing both the Senate Majority and Minority leader agree on is that I have no business in politics."

"Let me take care of Steve," Daniel said.

Mel poked him with her elbow. "I told you, no knocking people off."

He chuckled. "No problem. I'll send him to Rochester for a few days. There's a company that wants to open a plant on the outskirts, and current laws don't allow them to open there. They'll invite him for a tour after I talk to my friend on the board of directors. He'll go."

"Perfect. Thank you!"

"You're the best." Mel kissed him softly, then turned back to the camera. "What can I do?"

"For now? Have some faith in me. I'm so sorry I caused this problem. I'll never forgive myself if I can't fix it."

Her face turned serious. "I've always had faith in you, Lana. That's why I recommended you for this gig in the first place."

Tears prickled at the corners of my eyes. "I'm so sorry I let you down."

"You could never let me down," Mel said. "There's a reason we've been best friends since high school. You stopped the other kids from bullying me. You encouraged me to be myself, to follow my dreams."

"Heh. Maybe I should've taken my own advice."

"What are you talking about?" she asked.

"Am I following my dreams? Or I am doing what I've always done? Floating along, attaching myself to whatever came up because it was easier than making a decision."

"Hiking into the woods to beg the governor to listen to you wasn't the easy way," Daniel pointed out. "You're stronger than you think."

"It's okay to take your time to find your place in the world," Mel said. "Isn't that what you told me? Instead of taking any crappy job I could find, you encouraged me to start my own studio."

"A studio I accidentally arranged to shut down."

"Is this a pity party?" Mel asked. "Because I don't do pity

parties. You've got a chance to fix things here. Are you going to do it, or are you going to feel sorry for yourself?"

She was absolutely right. I'd made a mistake, but I was in a position to make everything better. She was the one on the verge of losing everything. Sure, I'd invested the cash, but that meant nothing compared to destroying my most important relationship. Mel didn't feel sorry for herself, and neither would I.

I sat up straight. "Thanks for the kick in the pants. I've got work to do."

By the time we hung up, my coffee pot was beeping the "done" signal, and I was fired up. I poured a steaming mug of hazelnut coffee with generous amounts of milk and sugar, then sat down and got to work.

The next morning, I went straight to Minority Leader Rumsfeld's office and found Gretchen in the middle of a call. She hung up hurriedly when I entered. "What do you need?"

I didn't beat around the bush. "Governor Abbot is going to veto the Schools Zoning and Protection Act. She wants us to rewrite it without the clause giving communities the right to ban certain types of businesses based on their religious views."

Gretchen smirked. "Whatever. We'll get the votes to override."

"Not so fast," I said. "I'm not voting to override. And neither will most of the other Democrats once I finish talking to them."

The smile fell off her face. "What are you talking about? You voted in favor."

"Yes, I did. Because you lied about the contents."

"I never lied," she said.

"'Oh, it's a routine bill,'" Judging by the grimace on her face, Gretchen didn't appreciate my impression of her. "If I recall correctly you said, 'It'll pass easily, a rubber stamp.'"

She folded her arms across her chest. "That was before the

latest round of revisions. To be honest, I'm surprised you voted in favor. So was everyone else."

My temper flared at the reminder of how Steve played me, but I forced myself to remain calm. "No one told me they moved the vote up. I suppose I have you to thank for that?"

She shook her head. "No, that's not my job. Senator Rumsfeld's assistant handles notifications and reschedules. You should have gotten an email Thursday afternoon. It was late, but unless you left early, you would have seen it."

"Hold on a sec. How late?"

"Like four-thirty or so? I'd have to check."

Right around the time Steve appeared in my office with iced coffee but "forgot" the straw. I wonder how he convinced Linda to go get it herself instead of sending him. I didn't doubt for a second that he found and deleted the message while we were both out of the office. What a sleaze.

Still, he had to have known what time to go in there.

I eyed Gretchen carefully. "What is your relationship with Steve?"

"It's none of your business."

"You're right. And I don't care. I just hope you're not sleeping with him."

She gasped. She tried to cover it with a cough, but her anger was apparent. "Get out of my office."

"Gladly," I said. "I have work to do. The Schools Zoning and Protection Act is going down."

The sound of a drawer slamming open was my only response. I was halfway to the door when I heard a soft grunt of pain. She tried to cover it up, but something was wrong. Although part of me wanted to keep going and pretend I hadn't heard anything, it wasn't in my nature to ignore someone who was hurting just because I didn't like her.

Gretchen stood at her desk, struggling to pull something out of the bottom drawer. Whatever it was must be stuck. As I watched, her hands slipped, and she smacked herself in the forehead. Her face turned bright red.

"Why are you still here?"

"Let me help." She flinched but reluctantly stepped aside. Inside the drawer, the file she wanted was wedged under a mass of other documents. I pulled it out and handed it to Gretchen without looking inside.

"I loosened it for you," she said. I chuckled, and she begrudgingly cracked a smile. "Thanks."

For the first time, I took a good look at her. Thinning hair, shadows under her eyes. I'd thought she worked too many hours but combined with her getting out of breath and seeming too weak to wrestle a document out of her drawer, I wondered if she were ill. Especially since she'd been on leave right before I started. None of my business, but I had to ask. "Are you okay?"

"Fine," she snapped.

"I've got some stress balls to help with grip in my office if you want. They help."

"Part of the stripper trade?" Sarcasm dripped from her voice.

Whatever. If that was how she wanted to play it, she could sit in her office and be nasty alone. I rolled my eyes. "Sorry for helping."

My hand was on the doorknob when she spoke again. "Why don't you ever say anything to dispel the stripper rumors?"

I thought about leaving. Or about turning and letting her have it. Instead, I took a deep breath and turned to face her. "Because it doesn't matter. I'm smart, I'm a hard worker, and to be honest, if people would give me a chance, I could be awesome at this job. I made one mistake, largely because I didn't know the hearing got moved. I hate slut-shaming, and I hate that stripping is tied to slut-shaming. But arguing with people won't make them open their minds. I need to show them what I can do.

"I'm done waiting for people to give me a chance to make a difference. It's time for me to make my own chance. And to start, I'm getting the Schools Zoning and Protection Act vetoed and replaced. With or without your help."

Without waiting for a response, I turned and marched down the hall.

My next stop should have been to see Jason. Truly it should. But I didn't. I turned and walked in the opposite direction, toward my own office. I may be a newbie around here, but I knew freedom of expression inside and out. I knew how to negotiate. If I wanted people to take me seriously, I needed to take a stand rather than asking someone else to speak for me.

"Hi, Linda," I said to my assistant the moment the door closed behind me. "I need a list of everyone present for the Schools Zoning and Protection Act vote, how they voted, their email addresses, and phone numbers. Senate and Assembly."

Her eyes widened. "Does this mean what I think it means?"

"It means we're not out of this thing yet." I started toward my office. "Hold all my calls, please. If anyone other than Jason calls or shows up, tell them I'm out."

"You got it." She smiled at me. "I'm proud of you."

"Not so fast. I haven't done anything yet."

"But you will. You can do anything once you set your mind to it."

"You know I can't give you a raise because you butter me up," I teased.

"I do. I also know deflection is a way of protecting your heart," she returned. "You forget; we've worked together for years. I saw all the long hours you put in behind the scenes, repairing Mel's image and helping her campaign."

I glanced around as if someone else might overhear. "Shh! That's supposed to be our secret."

"That's my point," she said. "You're selfless, you work your butt off, and you get results. Now get to work while I make that list. My boss has to make the world a better place."

Chapter Twenty-One

The next morning dawned way too soon. I'd been up all night doing research and making notes. If I was going to draft a new bill, get it to a vote, and get the legislature to approve it, all in the next eight days, there was no time to waste. I normally didn't eat much for breakfast, but lack of sleep always made me hungry. Rather than bolting a bowl of cereal before leaving home, I grabbed a breakfast burrito and coffee in the cafeteria.

The greasy food sat heavily in my stomach when I returned to my office, still reading, researching, and taking notes. The morning flew by. Before I knew it, I found myself with the rest of the Senators, filing into the chamber for the morning's session. Part of me wanted to skip it, but if I'd learned nothing else in the past week, it was that I had an obligation to know what was going on around me. I needed to stay educated and not count on anyone else to fill me in.

Even with nothing seemingly important having been scheduled for the day, anything could come up. Someone might have important commentary on something I stupidly thought was unimportant. Or a vote might have gotten rescheduled. You know, again. If I survived this mess, I vowed to find a way to stop people from hiding nasty clauses in innocuous bills. This behavior needed to stop. The people of New York deserved better than members of the legislature who snuck around and stabbed each other in the back while also screwing over large parts of the population.

Once everything on the agenda was finished, the Majority Leader asked if anyone wanted to discuss anything new. I could barely breathe, but I raised my hand and waited my turn. A few other people had things to talk about, so it took longer than I expected. Finally, though, she got to me.

"The Leader recognizes the Senator from Saratoga Springs."

I stood up too fast, and the contents of my stomach rolled. Oh, man. That breakfast burrito tasted much better the first time. Biting back a wave of nausea, I closed my eyes and waited.

"Senator Chen? Did you have something to discuss with this body?"

My eyes landed on Jason, which was the last place they should be. He never called or texted me over the weekend, probably because *his wife* wouldn't have liked it. Fine with me. I didn't have any time for cheaters. Mel's ex cheated on her during their entire relationship, and she largely ignored the signs. The day they finally broke up, I wanted to throw a parade.

The memory made me smile, helped me gather my wits enough to focus on what I needed to say. I sipped my coffee, hoping that would help. Instead, an angry howl emitting from my stomach. It sounded like someone had let a sick cow into the room. A few titters sounded from the audience.

Lovely. Just what I needed.

Gritting my teeth, I forced myself to power through my prepared comments. "Good morning, Majority Leader Diaz.

Good morning, Senators. Last week, as you know, this body voted to pass the Schools Zoning and Protection Act by a narrow margin."

"Yes, Senator Chen, I believe you tipped the scales in favor of the bill. Without you, it would've failed. Thanks for the reminder. Are you intending to gloat?"

I shook my head emphatically. "No, ma'am. After the vote, I discovered provisions had been added to the bill after the draft I read. Provisions that changed everything."

"I'm sorry, but there's no way to rescind your vote."

"I know. However, Governor Abbot has agreed to veto the bill, if we can pass something similar without the restrictions on freedom of expression. Today, I want to let you know I intend to introduce the Miller Act. This new legislation will strengthen existing zoning provisions while not allowing anyone to object to the placement of a business that has received appropriate permitting based on their personal, moral, or religious views."

Beside Majority Leader Diaz, Minority Leader Rumsfeld jumped to his feet. "This is outrageous!"

"Excuse me, sir, but I believe you're out of order." I'd always wanted to say that. Unfortunately, neither Rumsfeld nor Diaz looked amused.

"Senator Chen, I believe I'm the one with the gavel," she said. "Minority Leader Rumsfeld, did you have something to add?"

"You know I do," he said. "This bill was voted on last week. It passed with more than fifty percent of the vote. There is no provision for amending it now."

"Yes, I'm aware of that," I said. "But we can pass another law, a better one."

"Why on earth would we do that?"

"I'm inclined to agree with Minority Leader Rumsfeld." Majority Leader Diaz pressed her lips together, clearly frustrated. "Senator Chen, I'd remind you that this is the state legislature, not a three-ring circus."

It was on the tip of my tongue to point out that the two weren't terribly different, but I suspected no one here would appreciate my jokes. "I'm sorry, Majority Leader. But the Miller Act is important. The Schools Zoning and Protection Act started out great, then went bad. The amendments added provisions at the last minute that will strip women of their rights to free expression and their right to earn a living."

As soon as the word "strip," left my mouth, I wanted to pull it back. Not the time to remind the entire chamber of mostly men about the rumors. Suddenly, I had no doubt most of them were picturing me without clothes. My stomach gurgled, and I clenched my butt cheeks together. I desperately needed to get to the nearest restroom, and thanks to these interruptions, my entire speech wasn't going to come out first.

"Come out" also not a great phrase at the moment, as I worried that the bacon grease and cheese from my breakfast might start seeking an exit if I didn't get out of here soon. But I held the floor, sort of, and I hadn't finished my speech yet.

Bravely, I forced myself to shoulder on. "This is unacceptable. And it never should have happened. One of the proponents of the Schools Zoning and Protection Act prevented me from discovering that the vote had been moved. I never got a chance to review the final amended text."

"What are you saying? You didn't read the bill before you voted in favor of it?"

My face burned so brightly, you could see it from space. I longed for the floor to open up and swallow me. "Yes, ma'am. And while I realize it is my fault the Schools Zoning and Protection Act passed, I have an opportunity to right that wrong. It hasn't been made the law yet. I've been up all night, working on the Miller Act. I'm prepared to present it to you this afternoon. It has all the same substantive provisions as the original act, minus the slut-shaming."

"Excuse me, Majority Leader Diaz, but I object!" Rumsfeld let out a strangled sound, and I wondered if it was due to his outrage at the Miller Act or frustration over having to address someone else as "majority leader." "I don't know what kind of behavior Senator Chen is used to in the strip clubs, but we don't have a refund policy here. Perhaps she should stick to sleeping with married men and let the real legislators pass the laws."

Someone gasped, but I didn't see who. It was the first time anyone brought up the rumors about me on the Senate floor. Murmurs erupted all around the room. I needed to say something, anything, to bring the discussion back on track.

Stomach cramps caused me to double over in pain. This was not the time. Why, oh, why, did I choose this morning of all days for a greasy breakfast on top of no sleep?

I opened my mouth to object, but Jason stood instead. "Majority Leader Diaz, I move to strike Minority Leader Rumsfeld's comments from the record as defamatory."

"Motion granted. Senator Chen, do you have anything else you want to say?" Majority Leader Diaz asked.

The strain of holding everything back made me taste blood. And I was fighting a losing battle, anyway. The gas in my stomach wanted out, and it only had two potential exits. There were many, many things I wanted to say in response to Rumsfeld's sexist and derogatory comments. I was a Yale-educated lawyer! Unfortunately, as everyone's attention turned back to me, only one sound filled the room: the slowly explosive sound of gas being released from a balloon. Only it wasn't coming from a balloon. It was coming out of the back of my tailored suit skirt, and no matter how hard I clenched, I couldn't stop it.

A huge, booming laugh filled the chamber. Rumsfeld. To

my horror, another laugh followed, and soon the sound filled
the room. Even the chairwoman struggled to keep a straight
face. I couldn't stand the thought of looking at Jason. If he
were laughing at me, too, I'd never be able to walk into this
room again. I couldn't do this. What had I been thinking? This
was all a huge mistake.

With tears streaming down my cheeks, I turned and ran
from the room. Steve had been right. I was no state Senator. I
was a joke.

Chapter Twenty-Two

When Gretchen arrived in my office twenty minutes later, I was busy throwing all the meager belongings from my desk into my purse. She watched me for a moment before speaking. "So that's it? You're giving up?"

"What does it matter? All I've done since I got here was mess things up. I ruined my best friend's career, and you saw what happened in there. I'm a punchline. No one has any respect for me or my opinions. They're never going to pass the Miller Act, not now."

She pulled up a chair. "Mind if I sit?"

"Do you need to sit to gloat?"

"I'm not here to gloat. I want to help."

Yeah, right. Help me pack? Sitting down with Gretchen listening to her attack everything I believed in sounded about as much fun as a root canal. Standing here and arguing sounded even less fun. Maybe if I let her say her piece, she'd leave.

I let out a sigh, still packing. "Fine. What's up?"

"You did it," she said. "You've convinced me to help. The Miller Act is going to pass. I'll make sure of it."

"That's not funny."

"No, listen. This isn't a joke. I watched your video. Three times."

"Oh yeah? Do you have some cutting jabs to make about my appearance?"

"I was going to say, 'Wow, what an amazing show of strength.'" She shrugged. "But if you want me to comment on your appearance, those shoes were gorgeous."

For the first time, I smiled at her. "Thank you."

"That got me thinking, wondering. But now—I'm on your side. What Rumsfeld did to you on the floor today was inexcusable."

My heart jumped into my throat. For the first time since she entered my office, I stopped moving around and actually looked at Gretchen. "Are you serious? Not that I want to argue, but I've had a terrible day, and I'm not sure I can handle more."

"Yeah, I saw. Listen. I thought about the things you said. I mean, I don't buy into all your rah rah women sisterhood crap." She rolled her eyes. "But I also don't believe in ridiculing someone for being a woman, or for falling for the wrong guy. Nothing that's happened in the past two weeks was your fault. Steve was playing you all along."

I flushed and averted my eyes. "How did you know?"

"Because I overheard Rumsfeld talking to him yesterday. They knew it was going to be a close vote. They know Curtis would have gone along with it if he'd been elected, and they knew you wouldn't. Not if you had time to read and think about it before the vote."

"Yup. Still, I should've read it."

"And maybe you would have, if he had told you that the vote was moved. That's why he showed up with the iced coffee, you know. Forgetting the straw was no accident. He needed to get your secretary out of the way so he could delete the email before she spotted it."

"I knew it!" I shook my head. "I can't believe I was so stupid."

"Just be glad you had the good sense not to go home with him. I believe his original plan was to keep you up all night so you'd oversleep."

I shuddered. "You know, I'm not surprised. But thank you for confirming he's even more of a creep than I thought."

She cleared her throat. "You're welcome. I, uh, may also have learned about him the hard way."

For the first time since we met, I felt a kinship with Gretchen. "Oh, no. I'm sorry. He wanted your vote?"

"He wanted me to forge Rumsfeld's name on a job recommendation. Which is ludicrous. No one is good enough in bed for me to tank my career. Probably not even Chris Evans. Especially not Steve." She cleared her throat. "Anyway, it's all in the past. Let's talk about the Miller Act."

"You mean the Act that got me laughed off the Senate floor? Thanks, but I was thinking instead I'd go home and never come back."

"Well, you can't do that," she said. "It'll start a rumor that Saratoga Springs's seat is cursed."

"Maybe it is." I sighed. "All I wanted was to help people."

"It's not too late," she said. "Listen, after you raced out, there were some other comments before Majority Leader Diaz shut everything down. A lot of them were unkind, and I won't repeat them, but they made me think. All my choices in life led me here, to this job. I love my job. I'm happy with the choices I made—but I was fortunate to have plenty of options. Some people don't."

"Careful. Words like that, you sound like a liberal."

She gasped and clasped her hands over her chest. "The horror!"

As much as I appreciated what Gretchen was telling me, this all sounded too easy. Why would she get me bill signers? I mean, yes, I made good points, but there had to be something more. She'd been working as Rumsfeld's Chief of Staff for too long to secretly oppose all his views. "Thank you so much. I truly appreciate it. But why would you help me?"

"You helped me," she said. "For no reason."

"I helped you because you needed it."

"Exactly. That's who you are." She paused. "Jason showed me your rough draft of the Miller Act. You did a good job, especially for your first effort."

Her words lifted my spirits for the first time all morning. "Thanks, but if I hadn't screwed everything up in the first place, I wouldn't have needed to do any of this."

"Be that as it may, it takes a big person to admit her mistakes. And an even bigger one to do something about it."

In response, I smiled. "That's the nicest thing you've ever said to me."

"I've given Rumsfeld my notice," Gretchen said. "Seeing as how I'm going to have a lot of free time on my hands, I'd like to volunteer for your office."

I choked, spewing coffee everywhere. Including across the desk, onto her white shirt. Hurriedly, I grabbed a bunch of napkins and started blotting. "I'm so sorry."

She laughed. "Maybe I should have better prepared you."

"I can't have heard you right."

"You did. What happened today made it glaringly obvious that I can't continue to work for him," she said. "I always knew he was sexist, but this was the last straw. At the Christmas party last year, I overheard him telling Senator Kavanagh he only hired me because of my hot ass."

I gasped. "He didn't."

"He did. Sadly, I wasn't even surprised. I'd suspected, but I didn't want to know. I wanted to believe he hired me because of my resume."

"I'm sure he did," I said. "Your resume had to get you in the door before he could have any idea of, er… your other assets."

She smiled thinly. "It doesn't matter now. At the time, I shrugged it off. Told myself he only said it because he was drunk, and that he respected me as an employee. But I'm done shrugging things off."

"I couldn't agree more. So you left Rumsfeld?"

"Yup. I presented him with a copy of the Miller Act, told him it's time to pursue my own agenda, and laid my resignation letter on top."

Hold on a sec. Was she saying what I thought…? "Your own agenda? You're going to run against him."

She held up one hand. "Not so fast. I am thinking about running for office one day, but not yet. Also, not against Rumsfeld. I found a gorgeous farmhouse, and it's in an adjacent district. Until then, I'd like to gain some experience working to support women for a change."

"Good for you. And you really want to help me with this bill?"

"I do," she said. "I think we'll push each other to be our best. That doesn't mean I agree with all your politics. It means you've opened my eyes to some things I once preferred to ignore. You've inspired me. I want to fight for a change. Make the world better, based on my ideals—not Rumsfeld's."

"A brilliant plan," I said.

A voice in the back of my head made me wonder if this was all another scheme that she concocted with Steve. I wanted to trust Gretchen, and the things she said rang true, but my gut had been letting me down lately.

"So I can be your volunteer?" she asked.

"No." I shook my head. "Sorry, but I'm not looking for any volunteers at the moment."

Her face fell. "I understand. I—"

"I want you to be my Chief of Staff." If Gretchen was telling the truth, the Miller Act's chances of passing shot up significantly in the past five minutes. I could use her, but I wasn't going to make her work for free.

She blinked at me repeatedly. "You want to give me a job?"

"I do. You're smart, competent, and I hear you run a tight ship, which is exactly what I need around here. You'll keep me on my toes, and you won't agree with me just for the sake of agreement."

"I can pretty much guarantee it."

I laughed. "Think about this as a trial offer. Before I can hire anyone to work for me, I have to know that I can trust them. But I need your help. You can start immediately. Let's get this bill to bed and bring home the votes we need. Then we'll talk about making your position permanent."

"Deal."

With Gretchen's unexpected assistance, the days until the vote flew by. We reached out to Senators and Assembly Members on both sides of the aisle. Every single member of both houses got phone calls, emails, arguments. Gretchen and I tag-teamed them, switching back and forth as necessary. Making points and counterpoints. We stressed the importance of putting aside petty differences to come together on the big issues, like the First Amendment. We ordered pizza and kept the phone lines going. Linda helped, updating the giant white-board I'd brought in after every call and making detailed spreadsheets. Slowly but surely, we would make this happen.

By four o'clock Monday, we'd managed to gather promises of support from more than two-thirds of the members of both houses. I couldn't believe it. When Gretchen gave me the news, I shrieked with joy. "You're serious? We did it?"

"You did it," she said. "Not just a majority. It's veto-proof."

My scream of pure joy filled the room. There was no better way to send Governor Abbot a message that I'd taken her words to heart and decided to fight for what I believed in. Even knowing she planned to sign the Miller Act, realizing it would become law either way felt amazing.

"Thank you so much, Gretchen. Truly, I couldn't have done this without you." Impulsively, I hugged her. "Now go home and rest. I've got a few things to finish up here."

"Thanks. And don't stay all night. You need to rest, too."

She was right, but before I left, there was more work to do. I read and re-read the bill to make sure there were no hidden loopholes. Part of me still worried this was an elaborate trick and Gretchen had snuck more secret text in. But at seven-thirty, when Linda printed out the last draft, we were the only two people left in the building. I told her to go home and spend the rest of the evening with her daughter, who was visiting from out of town. Instead, she read the final version of the Miller Act aloud to help me find any typos. I listened with my eyes shut, savoring the fruits of my labor. The bill was perfect. I staggered into bed shortly after midnight, exhausted but happy.

The next morning, I dressed carefully for the session, aware all eyes were going to be on me. Not just the other members of the Senate, but spectators and the viewers at home. Cable access would be filming us. Pushing past my rows of navy and black clothes, I found the bright red suit I'd only worn a couple of times. It was one of the first suits I'd sewn, made for the final presentation of my college speech and debate class. I got it because the fabric was so cheap, it wouldn't matter if I messed it up.

But I hadn't. I'd added pleats to the skirt and a fun lining, and it was one of my favorite pieces of clothing. I rarely wore it because my natural inclination had always been to fade into the background. Not today. This suit was fun and feminine and eye-catching, and that was what I wanted.

A patterned blouse and black high heels completed the look. Then I applied my makeup carefully and studied the results. I looked like a strong, capable woman who was not to be forked with. Perfect.

This time, I arrived at my office more than an hour before the vote. Too nervous to sit or drink coffee, I did lunges back and forth across the floor until Linda came in to insist I eat something. Something *not* greasy, that would not make me sick on the floor of the senate. I refused until she shoved a piece of toast in my mouth.

Twenty minutes before roll call, I gathered my things and headed to the chamber. I sat in my seat and held my head erect, facing forward. No one was going to get in my way this time. After Majority Leader Diaz called the session to order and finished the roll call, her eyes landed on me.

"The first matter on the agenda is Senate Bill 4379, the Miller Act. This has been fast-tracked through the committees to get to the full chamber. Does anyone have any final comments before we vote?"

I raised my hand, awaiting recognition. The majority leader acknowledged me, and I stood. The floor was mine.

"Good morning, Majority Leader Diaz. As you know, I am Senator Lana Chen, author of the Miller Act. I've spoken to most of you personally, but I do have a few comments for the rest of the chamber and for the audience—both here in the balcony and anyone watching at home."

"You may proceed, Senator," she said.

"I haven't been working here long. My predecessor left unexpectedly, under very odd circumstances. My election was unorthodox at best. I knew that coming in. You all know it, too." I took a deep breath. "But what most of you don't know, because you never bothered to talk to me, is that I was born and raised on a series of military bases. I've lived in eleven different countries and multiple states. Eventually, my parents settled in Albany because my grandmother was sick."

"I don't see what this has to do with the bill," Rumsfeld interrupted.

"If you let me finish, you'll find out," I said. "When you all say I don't believe in family values, it hurts. I'm standing here today because of a woman who has been like a sister to me. I went to law school because I wanted to make the world a better place for the children I hope to have one day. Family is extremely important to me. But it's not as important as the Constitution.

"The First Amendment to the United States Constitution gave us all certain freedoms. The New York Constitution repeats those rights. The Schools Zoning and Protection Act tried to take freedom of expression away from people in general, and women specifically. I did the research, and if Governor Abbot signs the SCZPA into law, it's primarily businesses owned by women that will be negatively impacted. It's women working as dancers and fitness instructors. That's not acceptable. The Miller Act is a replacement, a new law Governor Abbot can sign instead." I took a sip from my water bottle, trying to gauge the reaction my words were having on the crowd. My peers were pretty good at hiding their emotions, though. Most of the room sat poker-faced. "It has come to my attention that some people want to vote against this new bill because rumor has it Governor Abbot will sign the SZPA if the Miller Act doesn't pass. Don't let that happen. The Miller Act includes all of the same basic zoning regulations as the Schools Zoning and Protection Act. It protects businesses from being targeted and closed due to slut-shaming. If you care about the people of New York, care about all residents. Please vote aye to remind the world that New York is a safe haven for anyone who comes within our borders."

"Thank you, Senator Chen." Majority Leader Diaz did not appear to be remotely moved by my passion. Hopefully others felt differently. "If that is all, it's time to vote. District 1, how do you vote?"

"Aye."

Just like that, we were off. A bomb couldn't have drawn me away from the room. My eyes glued themselves to each senator in turn. I tallied the votes myself, never even glancing down at my paper. This was too important. The Miller Act needed to pass, and it deserved one hundred percent of my attention.

When my turn came, I voted "aye" in a loud, clear voice, feeling the weight of that single word more than at any other time in my entire life. This wasn't about one bill. It was about standing up for equal rights.

Majority Leader Diaz continued around the room. Before she reached the last Senator, I knew what would happen. I held my breath, terrified if I breathed, something would go horribly wrong.

When the results were finally announced, a whoop of joy escaped me. Not just a majority. Not just a veto-proof majority. The Miller Act passed by an overwhelming majority. Almost everyone in the room voted in favor. I couldn't believe I'd done it!

Everyone turned to look, and I clapped my hand over my mouth. Oops. Then, on the side of the room, Gretchen started clapping. She stepped away from the wall, coming into full view of the chamber. Someone else started clapping, then a third. Senator Tulloss rose to her feet. Before I knew it, the entire legislature was giving me a standing ovation.

Okay, Rumsfeld crossed his arms and leaned back in his chair, but still. Not my problem. I grinned and waved at him.

"Thank you, everyone!"

It was time to call Mel and let her know we'd won. The newly revised bill would go straight to the Assembly, and they should vote immediately after lunch. People said the wheels of government turned slowly, but with the right oil, things got done fast. With any luck, the ink on Governor Abbot's signature would be dry by the time I arrived at Push and Pole Fitness for my first private lesson at the new location. Even though I'd told Mel not to continue moving toward the opening until she saw what happened, she'd refused to give up on me.

And the first amendment right to freedom of expression would be safe. For now, anyway, and hopefully for as long as I remained a member of the New York Senate.

I didn't walk to my office; I danced. People thought I was quirky? Let 'em look.

Chapter Twenty-Three

By the time I got off the phone with Mel, my stomach was growling. Good thing Linda made me eat this morning, or I never would have made it. My watch told me it was after one, which explained a lot.

This day wasn't over yet. Time to grab a sandwich and get back to work.

All thoughts of food fled my mind as soon as I stepped through to the outer office.

Gretchen's new desk sat empty, no surprise since she was taking a long lunch to celebrate our victory. Linda sat in her usual spot, but she wasn't alone. A girl with red rings around her gorgeous blue eyes sat on the chair normally reserved for people waiting to see me, which had been moved behind the desk. She appeared to be a couple of years younger than me, but I wasn't sure. Maybe the aura of sadness surrounding her made her seem childlike, almost fragile.

When I entered, Linda looked up. "Lana, this is my daughter Grace. Grace, this is Lana, our senator extraordinaire."

"Hi, Grace, it's nice to meet you." She didn't move or even

look at me, so I racked my brain to think what I could remember. "You're from Ohio, right? Are you visiting long?"

In response, she let out a wail and tore out of the room, a cloud of blond hair streaming behind her. Uh-oh.

"Was it something I said?"

"Oh, dear." Linda wrung her hands. "I should've warned you. Grace's husband threw her out. Took everything, including their dog. She's come to Albany to stay with me until she gets back on her feet."

Well, I'd put my foot into it. "I'm so sorry. I didn't know."

"It's not your fault. I brought her here because I thought she could use a friend, someone around her own age." She hesitated. "To be honest, I thought maybe you could try to get her into your friend's studio. My girl needs to regain her confidence, and pole classes are the way to do it."

"That's a great idea," I said. Lunch could wait. "Why don't you call Mel and set something up? The studio's not officially opening for a couple more weeks, but she can do private lessons. I'll let her know to expect to hear from you."

Linda shook her head. "Grace won't go if it's my idea. I was hoping you could draw her out, invite her."

That made sense. Theoretically, a heart-broken twenty-something would be more likely to listen to a friend than her mother. Unfortunately, I wasn't either at the moment. I tapped my finger against my lips thoughtfully. "What did she do in Ohio? For work."

"Customer service, mostly. She answered phones in a call center."

"Is she looking for a job?"

Linda's hands went to her hips. "Yes, but she can't have mine!"

I laughed. "I would never replace you. After all, you're the only person who understands the filing system around here."

"And I'll never tell you the secret." Her lips twitched. "If you haven't figured out yet that it's the alphabet, chances are my job is safe."

"Your job is safe because you're an utter delight, and you know it," I said. "No, I was thinking Mel could use someone at Push and Pole Fitness a few evenings a week. Answer the phone, go through the mail, take pictures for social media. Stuff like that."

"Grace could absolutely do that. You're a lifesaver, you know."

I shook my head. "I wouldn't go that far. First, let's see if I can even find out where she went."

The halls of the statehouse had become as familiar to me as the back of my hand over the past few weeks, but I remembered well how easy it was to get lost. Especially if you didn't want to be found. My first stop was the restroom, but as the one nearest my office was a single stall, it was easy to see from the open door that Grace wasn't there.

Beyond the restroom lay the other offices, most of which held closed doors. I imagined Grace wouldn't have taken refuge inside any of them. The maze of hallways continued to my right, but on a hunch, I turned left and went for the side door leading outside. If I were nursing a broken heart, I'd rather do it under the open sky than inside a three-hundred-year-old building full of strangers.

Outside, I breathed deeply and cleared my mind. The air was brisk, but not overly cold. Grace would be fine out here, but still, I wanted to find her. A flash of yellow caught my eye near a small copse of trees. Beyond the trees sat a bench, and a blonde figure huddled on the bench. The slump of her shoulders told me who it was, even if the hair hadn't given her away.

I approached slowly, as you might a scared rabbit. "Grace?"

"Go away. I don't want to talk to anyone."

"Okay, no problem. Can I sit?"

She eyed me warily. "It's a free bench."

Slowly, I turned and lowered myself, sliding down to rest my head on the back. Gazing up at the blue sky, I waited. It was one of those rare perfect April days. It was nice to be outside.

As always when I sat alone with my thoughts, my mind traveled to Jason. What a mess. Who was I to be offering advice to anyone? My love life was completely forked.

She eyed me from her side of the bench. "Are you okay?"

I heaved a sigh. "I'm supposed to be out here giving you advice. But I should clean my own house before criticizing yours."

Grace shrugged. "Sometimes it helps to talk about things. You want to vent, I'm here."

"It's not that easy. You first." I held up one hand. "Listen. Your mom's a good friend. You don't have to tell me anything you don't want. But her heart is in the right place, and I know all about getting screwed over. You tell me your story; I'll tell you mine."

Something glinted her in eyes. A moment later, she opened her mouth, and the words started pouring out. She'd met her husband in college (it didn't escape my notice she wasn't even referring to him as ex yet). He'd been perfect—everything she wanted. Friend, confidante, sounding board….the more she described him, the more he sounded like Steve. I knew what she was going through.

"I was so stupid," she moaned. "I let him talk me into moving to Ohio, where I didn't know anyone. And then he was my entire world. Between work and doing whatever he wanted, I had no time to make any friends. He and his friends were my life."

"So what happened?"

She sniffled. "We'd been trying to have a baby for a while now. Started almost as soon as we got married. I know some people say you should wait, but he's the real deal, right? I loved him, and I always wanted kids. I figured why not start trying immediately?"

Having never met anyone I wanted to procreate with, I didn't know how long you were supposed to wait before you started "trying." I always hated that euphemism. It was just like saying, "We're having a lot of sex," a visual I never needed. Which was inappropriate and off-topic. "Did the two of you have a baby?"

She shook her head. "After two years, I went to my doctor. Got a bunch of tests. Everything was fine. I passed with flying colors. Todd refused to get tested. But then… one of his friends told me the truth. He got a vasectomy. Years ago, right before we got engaged."

I gasped. "And he didn't tell you? That's fraud."

"I had no idea." She swallowed, and a tear trickled down her cheek. "That wasn't the worst of it, though. He'd been cheating on me the whole time. Moved back to Ohio so he could be closer to his high school sweetheart. Because he owned our house before we got married, he tossed me out. I didn't even get to say goodbye to our dog."

Oh, hashtag. What a horrible, horrible man. I couldn't even imagine how she must feel. No friends, no nearby family, no support group, no home, no baby—and no dog. Her husband had taken everything from her, and for his own selfish reasons.

Grace's story touched my heart. There might be ways I could help—and I intended to have a very long talk with Daniel about what those ways might be before I swallowed my pride and went to propose new legislation to Jason. That would take time, though. I had weeks of research ahead of me, looking into the best way to help not just Grace, but other women in her position. What was the recourse for women whose husbands took away their choices without telling them?

Grace was young, so she theoretically could still have kids, but what about women who didn't find out until it was too late?

"I'm so sorry," I said. "And I'm going to find a way to help."

"I appreciate that, but how? What can you do?"

Good question. What could I do? I was in a position to make a difference here, and I intended to figure out how to use it to my advantage. But first, Grace needed more than a shoulder to cry on. The longer we'd talked, the more I realized that suggesting we go to pole lessons together wasn't the way to get this woman out of her shell. Instead, I tried another tactic. "Well, to start. I can help you regain your independence. I know you're hoping not to be in town long, but I'm wondering if you might be interested in some part-time temporary work? A friend of mine just started a new business, and she could use someone to answer the phones."

"Why are you asking me?"

"Because you come highly recommended by one of the people I trust most in the world."

"Mom's biased."

"Fine, I'll check your references. But if you did telephone customer service before, you'll be fine." I waved one hand. "Look, my dad was in the military. I know what it's like to be in a strange place where you don't know anyone. I know what it's like to feel lost."

As she listened, I told Grace what had happened over the past few weeks, from the moment Mel asked people to write-in my name, up through the weekend. She sat silently until I finished.

"Wow. You're as messed up as I am," she said finally.

I laughed. It felt good. "I'm sorry, I don't know where that came from."

"Better out than in, I always say."

"Didn't Shrek say that?"

"Okay, yes, but it's still good advice. Also, I love that you know that," she said. "Full disclosure: I saw the newspaper article."

"You and the rest of the world," I grumbled. "At least the picture caught my good side."

"Mom was pissed. Anyway, it's good to remember there are two sides to every story. Does this guy know how you feel about him?"

"Who, Steve? I don't think I left much room for doubt."

She turned and looked me squarely in the eyes. Now that she was giving me advice, she looked much less fragile than she had in my office. Like the kind of woman who could tackle anything. She would get along well with Mel. "That's not who I meant and you know it."

I took a deep breath. "No, Jason doesn't know how I feel about him."

Someone cleared their throat behind us. Someone who sounded male. My heart stopped.

Grace tilted her head toward the trees behind the bench. "Unless I'm mistaken, he does now. Isn't that him?"

Chapter Twenty-Four

Her words froze me in place. No, this couldn't be happening. I couldn't move, couldn't breathe. Couldn't believe Jason overheard me pouring my heart out, telling Grace how I felt about him. After everything, I refused to let this added layer of humiliation be the next chapter of our story. Especially when, if things worked out as I hoped, we'd be working together for a very, very long time. As platonic friends, of course. I'd never wanted him to find out I had been developing romantic feelings for him. Not now.

Grace must be mistaken. With great trepidation, I craned my neck, scanning the surrounding area to figure out who she saw.

It didn't take long. Directly behind the bench, a path through the trees ended at a fountain. Jason stood at the edge of the path, looking thunderstruck. He must've been as surprised to hear my revelation as I was when Grace pointed him out.

How had I not noticed someone approaching? I'd been so caught up in Grace's story—and then in having a friend to talk to—that I completely forgot where I was. Out in the open, in a public place, at work. Three places *not* to confess a private crush on someone. Especially in a place when voices carried well. No way he missed hearing me.

My cheeks burned. Silently, I begged for the ground to open up and swallow me.

My new friend stood. "I've got to go find Mom. Thanks for the talk."

"Hold on, I'm coming with you."

"No, I'm fine," she said.

"Lana. Please stay." Jason spoke from behind me. I still hadn't managed to bring myself to look at him. "I didn't mean to eavesdrop. I couldn't help overhearing. And hoping."

I closed my eyes briefly, debating my options. I couldn't spend the next several months avoiding my mentor. Or years, if I won re-election. I couldn't drop out of the race because I was afraid of my feelings. We'd barely been anything. I'd move on.

Finally, I sighed. "Okay, I'll stay. Grace, get Mel's number from your mom before you leave."

She was gone practically before I finished the sentence. Traitor.

"You did good," he said.

"Thank you." I started down the hall toward my office. Jason fell into step beside me.

"Why didn't you tell me what you were doing? I could have helped."

"I know. And I thought about it, I did. Many times. But I wanted to prove I could do this by myself." *And I didn't want to be around you right now.*

He stopped and turned me to face him. "Was that it, or are you mad at me because of the newspaper article?"

"I knew you were married once. I didn't know you were

married still." My cheeks grew warm as I studied the tips of his shoes. Lovely brown leather. Shiny. "It doesn't matter. We're friends, right?"

"Right." He cleared his throat. "And as my friend, you should know my wife and I separated four years ago. I filed for divorce six months later, and we reached an agreement. Turns out, the court rejected the papers on a technicality, but we never got the notice. We'd both moved. Neither of us had any idea the divorce wasn't finalized."

Hopelessness raised its head at his explanation, but I needed to be sure. My heart couldn't take another disappointment. "So you're not working things out with her?"

His lips twitched. "She has a child with someone else, and is expecting a second, so I sincerely doubt the two of us would get back together even if I wanted to. Which I do not."

I looked into his eyes. "You didn't lie when you called her your ex-wife."

"Not intentionally. She's not a part of my life. I had no idea we were still legally married, and as soon as I saw the newspaper article, I called my lawyer. The papers have now been filed. The marriage will be formally dissolved in a few weeks." He took a deep breath. "Anyway, since you were so infatuated with Steve, I didn't think it mattered."

Right. Steve. Jerky Steve who blinded me not only to how horrible his bill was, but to Jason's amazing qualities. "I made a mistake."

"It's none of my business."

Of course not. Because we were friends. And he didn't have any interest in me. I nodded. "Thanks for telling me."

"You're welcome." He cleared his throat. "Anyway, again, good work today."

"Thanks," I said. "I've made a decision. I want to give this job everything I have. I'm going to pour all my time and energy into doing the best I can for the people of Saratoga Springs. I signed my interest in the studio over to Mel. I can't manage both right now, not well."

"What changed your mind?"

"Getting completely screwed over?" Jason looked so confused, I laughed. "I think I've found my cause. I want to stop legislators from writing pork into bills. No more adding unrelated clauses to make someone happy, or sneaking bits in that would never pass muster alone."

"You want to make sure no one else goes through what you went through," he said.

"No. I want to make sure no one else accidentally puts the livelihood of hundreds of thousands of children at risk." I shook my head. "Voting for the SZPA without knowing the full contents was unconscionable. I should have abstained. But that clause never should have been in there."

"I tried to warn you."

"I know. I should've listened to you. I should've listened to you about a lot of things."

"You mean Steve?"

"Well, yes. But also, when you started to tell me about your ex-wife. When you told me you had my back." I swallowed and met his eyes squarely. "I'm so sorry."

"Please believe I never meant to hurt you. I've liked you since the moment we met, and I thought you liked me. It hurt when you started spending time with Steve. Especially, well, you know."

"I'm so sorry. I wish I'd realized who he is sooner."

"Not that I'm glad he ditched you in the forest or sabotaged you, but I am glad you found out the truth."

"Thanks," I said. "I should have followed my heart. But you were my mentor, and it seemed like a mistake. I was so scared of making things awkward, I talked myself into missing out on something amazing."

A slow smile spread across his face. "I've missed you."

"I've missed you, too. There's no one else I'd rather be stranded in a snowstorm with. Or trek lost in the woods with. Or hold me after a long day." I stepped toward him. "Can you ever forgive me?"

"There's nothing to forgive," he said. "I understand why you backed away. But I swear, I never meant to deceive you. I haven't considered myself married in a very, very long time."

My smile could've powered the entire city. "So you're free?"

"I wouldn't go that far," he said. "It appears my heart has already been claimed. Turns out, I have completely fallen for someone fierce and strong, inside and out. One of the most beautiful women I've ever met."

It took every ounce of self-possession not to throw my arms around his neck and devour him. But a tiny voice reminded me that we were not only in public, but we were at work, and a massive scandal involving us broke about a week ago.

Instead, I grabbed his hand and led him back down the path, behind a large oak tree.

"Everything okay?" he asked.

"Perfect. Just making sure no one can see us."

Finally, I raised up and wrapped my arms around his neck. He lifted me off the ground, his lips meeting me halfway as he spun me around. I curled my fingers into the silky strands at the nape of his neck, marveling at my luck. After everything we'd been through, I couldn't believe Jason still wanted to be with me.

Several moments later, I paused for air and rested my forehead against his. Jason held me like I was something precious, a gift to be protected. I hoped he'd never put me down. "You were talking about me, right? Because if not, this is awkward."

He threw his head back and laughed. The most glorious sound I'd ever heard. "Yes, Lana Chen. I'm talking about you.

I like everything about you. I'm so glad you accidentally became a senator."

Acknowledgments

First and foremost, thank you to my amazing editor Jami Nord. This book is about forty thousand times better since you've read it. :-) Thanks to Victoria Cooper for this beautiful cover. Thank you to Kerry Maloney, Kara Reynolds, Farah Heron, Marty Mayberry, and Laura Brown for reading through and marveling at my myriad typos. Thank you to Tracie Banister for the two thousand hours of moral support and brainstorming. Thank you Marty for your help with formatting and listening to me whine, and everything else.

Always and forever, thank you to my amazing husband for believing in me. And thank you to my readers for your support.

I hope you enjoyed this book. If so, please consider leaving an honest review on Bookbub or with your favorite retailer.

Did you like this book? Sign up for my newsletter at www.lauraheffernan.com and get a FREE copy of *Time of My Life*, my gender-flipped Dirty Dancing reboot. Just a little gift from me to you.

She's a poor dance teacher. He's her rich student. If they can overcome their differences, this could be love.

Legend says everyone who boards the Oceanic Aphrodite finds love. Janey's on the ship to teach pole fitness, not for romance. Then she meets Frank. He's everything Janey isn't—refined, classy, rich—but his good looks and charm make him undeniably appealing. Unfortunately, he's also a passenger.

When Janey's partner can't perform in the end-of-cruise talent show, Frank offers to fill in. He's never done pole, so he's got to learn fast. As they grow closer, Janey finds herself hoping the legend is real—but if she gives in to temptation, she could be out of a job.

SIGN UP FOR MY MAILING LIST TO GET YOUR FREE COPY.

R *ight, left, up, swing left leg around, climb, fall backward, pause.* The steps for my doubles routine went through my head on repeat while I stood in line at security, waiting to go through the inspection point and board the Oceanic *Aphrodite*. For the first time, I'd be dancing the Talent Show finale at the end of the cruise, which needed to go flawlessly. My future depended on this event, so I practiced every possible second.

My toes tapped in time with my thoughts, probably making me look quite odd. Fortunately, I'd been sailing this cruise for months as part of the onboard entertainment. The officers working the line knew me, and they were used to watching me dance in line. Once I made it to the metal detectors, it should be smooth sailing. Pun intended.

Normally, staff boarded the ship the night before or early in the morning before any guests arrived. My cabin mate Penny and I had gotten special permission to spend the night off-ship, a privilege that likely wouldn't be repeated now that her guy problems made us two hours late. At least they'd agreed to let us on right after the VIPs so we could beat most of the regular passengers.

Beside me, Penny tapped away on her phone, her long dark hair forming a curtain over the device. "Why hasn't Robbie texted me back?"

"I'm sure you'll hear from him soon." I struggled to keep from revealing my true feelings on the subject. "Especially since he'll be on the ship. It's not like he can avoid you forever."

Her head shot up, brown eyes flashing. "You think he's avoiding me?"

In truth, yes, I did. But if I hadn't been distracted thinking about our upcoming performance, I would have found a nicer way to say so. Well, probably. I'd been trying to politely tell her what a creep Robbie was for weeks, and she hadn't listened. Maybe it was time to be more direct. "I think he enjoys the rich passengers who might further his career once he graduates. Rob's pretty clear on his priorities, and you're not one of them."

"Ouch." Her face twisted into a grimace. A pang hit me. "I hope you're wrong."

"So do I, Pen. So do I." Not knowing what else to say, I changed the subject. "I'm excited that Max is letting us do the finale this week."

"Oh, I know! It's going to be amazing! The guests won't know what hit 'em. Especially the stuffy old farts who think pole dancing is only for strippers."

Despite myself, I blanched.

A look of horror crossed her face. "Oh, no. I'm sorry, Janey."

She hadn't meant to insult me, but I'd learned pole while working strip clubs. The patrons loved blue-eyed blondes, so owners always wanted someone with my look.

"It's fine," I said, breaking the awkward silence.

If things went well this week, the two of us would be cemented as dancing partners for the next year of cruises or more. Each additional performance meant cash in our pockets. I could ignore one thoughtless comment in the interests of continuing to pay for my father's assisted living every month. Dad had nowhere else to go, especially since his disability left him unable to care for himself.

Needing to look at anything else, I turned to face the metal detectors separating us from the ship's boarding area. The line of people might as well be a wall. I shifted from one six-inch heel to the other, wondering what this week's hold-up was. Last week, a bride didn't understand why her father couldn't bring his actual guns to her "shotgun" wedding. The week before, a groom tried to bring a case of whiskey, which is against ship policy. Maybe we had a celebrity up ahead. They always slowed down security. Rumor had it that some famous baseball player was getting married onboard this week. I didn't follow sports, though, so unless he wore his uniform, I'd never know.

Craning my neck to see the inevitable shenanigans at the front of the line, I almost didn't hear the commotion behind me. A woman gasped, then a child cried out. I turned to see what was happening, a fraction of a second too late.

A man's voice yelled, "Look out!"

Seconds later, something shoved me from behind, hard. Stumbling, I wheeled my arms for balance. The heel cracked off my shoe. I tumbled to the ground, landing hard on my hip. Ouch. As a dancer, I'm no stranger to injuries, but that was going to leave a bruise. It stung, almost as much as the realization that I was going to have to replace my two hundred dollar Pleasers—and with no time to go shopping before we set sail, I'd have to do it at one of the ship's outrageously overpriced boutiques. Entertainment staff got a discount, but not nearly enough. Silently, I kissed this week's earnings good-bye. At least I didn't have to pay for my room, utilities, or food.

"Are you okay?" The same voice asked.

Blinking several times to clear the pain clouding my vision,

I looked up to see such a delicious-looking man bending over me, I wondered if I imagined him. Curly brown hair falling across his forehead, light brown eyes the color of a latte, high cheekbones, a strong nose, and perfect lips. This face belonged in a museum.

"Gorgeous," I said without thinking. Then I flushed. "I mean, yes. I'm okay. What happened?"

His lips twitched at my slip of the tongue. "Runaway baggage cart. You were nearly murdered by a wedding dress. What an unfortunate end for such a talented fidgeter."

"You saw me dancing?"

"I may have noticed you before the cart rolled away."

The admission made me smile. "Well, thanks. If you hadn't been here, I might have been flattened."

"Glad I could help." He held out a hand to pull me to my feet. Our eyes locked, and suddenly, I couldn't breathe. "I'm Frank."

"Janey. Nice to meet you." As perfected over the years, I kept my face and tone pleasant but not overly friendly. As hot as this guy was, passengers were strictly forbidden. I didn't want to spend the entire cruise wishing he wasn't. Dropping his hand, I moved away from him, back toward the line.

A wince of pain sent me looking for the nearest chair. The fall must've twisted my ankle, and I'd been too distracted by this man to notice. Frank had shifted away, following my lead, but now he returned to my side. "Are you okay?"

"It's nothing. I'll walk it off."

"Let me see."

"It's no big deal," I insisted. "I'm a dancer. Happens far more often than it should."

"That's unfortunate, but please let me see it. It's my fault you're hurt, and I'm a doctor."

"Don't worry about me. Penny, are you okay?"

My friend stood nearby, her face unreadable. "It missed me

by a mile. But I'm a little dizzy. I've got to go. I'll see you onboard."

Before I could tell her not to go call deadbeat Robbie again, she vanished in the direction of the women's restroom, one hand resting on her stomach. Poor thing. My friend needed me, and I wanted to go with her, but my throbbing ankle stopped me. I didn't want to spent more time falling under Dr. Frank's spell, but the line to get onto the ship—and to the infirmary—hadn't budged. Better to sit and let him check me out than stand in pain, balancing on a broken shoe.

Together, we hobbled to a bench near the entrance to the security line. It wasn't nearly as far away as it should have been after twenty minutes of waiting. I collapsed with a sigh. Then my eyes landed on something and I groaned. "Oh, no."

"What's wrong?" Frank asked.

"My carry-on is still in the line. I need to grab it before someone reports it to security as an unattended bag."

"Is it that green one?" He pointed at my battered duffel, now sitting a bit outside the line, probably pushed by an overeager passenger. "That's all you need for a week?"

The bag only contained a few things I'd taken to spend the night at my sister's apartment, playing dress-up with my five-year-old niece. Easily the best thing about having a home port in Miami. Everything else remained in the cabin Penny and I shared. This passenger didn't need to know that.

"Yeah."

"Don't move." He touched my shoulder as he walked away, sending an unexpected jolt of desire through me. Oh, no. The last thing I needed was to get involved with a passenger, and this one could be trouble.

As my savior walked away, I marveled at his straight back, the way he held his head erect. The man moved with confidence, but also an innate grace, like a cat. Or a dancer. He didn't walk, he glided across the floor. I also took in the lines of his windbreaker, the creases of his pants, the leather of the shoes molding to his feet perfectly. Dr. Frank was off-limits for more reasons than one. Rich men only ever wanted one thing from girls like me, and I wasn't in a position to give it.

A moment later, he returned, my bag slung over his shoulder. I thanked him, then lifted my injured leg to rest on top once he set it in front of me. The pain subsided, so I scooted down to rest my head on top of the bench. Perfect. Except for being late to work and the throbbing ankle.

"I'm going to check you out now, okay?"

It was on the tip of my tongue to mention that I'd been checking him out for the last five minutes, but flirting with passengers needed to remain subtler, more innocent. I nodded. His touch was firm, yet soft. He poked and prodded for a moment while I did my best not to wince.

Finally, he said, "It's not broken."

Relief washed over me. If I broke my ankle, I'd be out of a job. While I loved my sister and niece, I didn't want to move in with them after becoming unemployed and homeless. "Thank goodness."

"Wrap it up for a couple of days, try to stay off it, and you should be fine. The infirmary will have elastic bandages."

"I've got one in my bag, actually," I said, opening a zipper on the side. "Part of the job."

"Excellent! Please, allow me."

I should say no, do it myself. After all, I'd wrapped various body parts a thousand times. But the smallest innocent touch couldn't hurt anything. His firm hands warmed my ankle, making it feel better already. Once we got on the ship, I'd never see him again. "Thanks."

He took the bandage and expertly wrapped my ankle in a matter of seconds. His hand lingered, just enough for me to notice. This magnetic pull between us wasn't one-sided. "There you go."

For the first time, I noticed how close he stood. The heat of his breath washed over my cheek. My skin burned where he'd examined my ankle. I refused to let myself wonder what these fingers would feel like moving over the rest of my body. He licked his lips, and my eyes darted involuntarily to follow the movement. I became helpless to look away.

It had been a long time since I'd been with anyone. Too long. I made a mental note to find a suitable hookup at the first port. Suitable meaning not a passenger, and not while on the ship. Not if I wanted to keep my job, which I very much enjoyed.

"Are you part of the Sassy Singles?" I asked, naming a group that booked multiple activities for passengers interested in meeting someone.

"Me? No, I'm not looking for a relationship." Good. Neither was I. Not that it mattered. He continued. "But it cracks me up that they'd put a singles cruise on a ship called the *Aphrodite*."

"Well, legend has it that people fall in love on this ship. One day, and you'll meet your mate. Or so they say."

"Huh. Good thing I believe in science over myth then."

"Yeah," I said, shaking off an inexplicable twinge of disappointment. The legend was a marketing ploy; all the staff knew it. After all, we'd been sailing around for months without falling in love. But it sold tickets for the singles cruises.

"Francis!" A high-pitched voice broke the spell between us.

Over the doctor's shoulder I spotted a stunningly gorgeous woman in flawless heavy makeup, chestnut hair with the top half twisted elegantly into a sleek chignon, and a swingy white sundress with big pink flowers painted all over it.

"Over here," he called to the woman.

"Francis, huh?"

"It's a family name."

"I'm sure it is." The longer we talked, the more dangerously close I came to crossing a line, but I couldn't resist one more comment before reining it in. "After the first woman in the cabinet?"

He grinned. "How'd you guess?"

The question was a joke, so his response startled me. I blinked a couple of times to cover my surprise before responding. "My mother was a big *Dirty Dancing* fan. I've got that and *Lethal Weapon* memorized."

What I didn't mention was that those were the only two videos we'd owned. After Mom walked out on me and my sister, those movies were my only way of feeling connected to her. I wore out the DVDs, watching them over and over.

"A woman of refined tastes," he said.

Before I could respond, the woman arrived at Frank's side, placing a perfectly manicured hand on his shoulder. She said nothing, her expression stormy, eyes hidden behind sunglasses the size of Disney World.

"Hey, Lisa," he said. "Is it time?"

"'Is it time?'" she mimicked, her face twisting into a grimace. "Duh! We're going to be late! Get your butt in line."

Girlfriend? Wife? No. No rings on either of them. My heart sank. Of course a man like Frank would have a girlfriend. Charming, sexy, rich, a doctor who moved with the grace of a dancer? The fact that I'd spent even half a second thinking he might be available made me flush with embarrassment. Especially when he'd said he wasn't looking for a relationship–he wouldn't be if he were here with someone.

On the other hand, this *was* a singles cruise, so maybe there was hope. The two of them had similar coloring, the same nose. As I took in the shapes of their faces, I'd bet my favorite Pleasers that she was related to Frank.

With a sigh, I glanced at my feet. Second favorite pair, anyway. These were toast.

"We can't be late. The ship isn't going to disembark with

VIP passengers waiting to go through the security line," he said, but he stood to follow her.

Of course he was a VIP. The sunglasses pushed casually on top of his head cost more than half my Pleasers collection. The shoes I needed for work and had been accumulating slowly over the past ten years, most of them from eBay. We didn't move in the same circles. I couldn't even afford to window shop in his world.

"What if it does, though? Won't you feel terrible?" She spoke slowly, as if addressing an unintelligent child. She must be an older sister; younger siblings never got away with talking like that. I had to believe Frank wouldn't date someone who treated him like something stuck to the bottom of her shoe. "I can't believe this. I should be sipping champagne right now."

I craned my neck up to meet her eyes from my seated posi-tion. "The VIP passengers are the first to board. You'll have over an hour to relax and explore the ship while the non-VIPs are going through security downstairs. Unless you turn around and leave the port area, you'll be fine."

"Thanks," the woman said icily. She gave me a practiced once over before turning back to Frank. "Who is this and why are you talking to her instead of going through security?"

"I'm Janey. I work–"

She put her hand out in the 'stop' sign. "That's nice. We have to go."

"So, uh, that's my sister," Frank said as Lisa stalked away. Unlike her brother, she moved like a linebacker.

"Seems delightful."

"Being late stresses her out. She's usually not so bad. Anyway, looks like we made it to the front of the line." A couple watched us from the space directly in front of the metal detectors as Lisa walked through. Frank gestured at them. "Those are my friends, Jake and Margie. Do you want to join us so you don't have to wait?"

From the other side of security, Lisa turned, hands on hips. "Francis Hanson, now!"

If the rest of his party was anything like her, the last thing I wanted was to hang out with them. "Thanks, but I'll wait for Penny. I don't want to get on your sister's bad side."

"You're right about that." He laughed. "I've got to go. Sorry."

"It's cool. Thanks again for saving me." Before I finished my sentence, he'd jogged off to meet his party.

Watching him go, I sighed. Well, it was a nice moment, before Lisa showed up. Probably for the best, given our circumstances.

I pulled myself upright, testing my sore ankle. Not terrible, not great. I was supposed to dance in this evening's welcome show, though, and that might not be possible.

Digging around in my bag, I found a pair of flip flops in the bottom. Switching shoes helped. Then I went to find Penny. She hadn't gone far, standing outside the bathroom near the row of pay phones. In all my months working for the cruise line, this was the first time I'd seen anyone looking like they might use one.

I didn't ask if she'd managed to get through to Robbie, preferring to believe she hadn't tried. I was afraid she used a pay phone to try to trick him into answering her call, which made me sad. Penny deserved so much better. At least she put her phone away and returned to the line with me.

The rest of the VIPs had finished going through security and waited for the gangway to open. Through the crowd, I spotted the captain's hat bobbing toward the giant glass doors. A glance at the clock on the wall told me he would be boarding soon, and this area would clear out quickly.

Scooping up my bag, I went through the line in record time. The throbbing in my ankle had dulled to an ache, and I thought about finding Dr. Frank to thank him again. Probably a bad idea, given the chemistry between us, but also the polite thing to do.

Then I spotted him, through the glass separating the waiting area from the docks. He walked about five steps behind the Captain. Beside him strode Lisa, the couple from the security line, and two people I recognized with a start. Only very special guests got priority boarding, which reinforced that this guy was way out of my league. But what sealed our lack of fate was the person who walked beside Frank's friend: my boss, Max Weiss.

Consorting with the passengers was strictly prohibited. If I did anything beyond extremely innocent flirtation with Frank, and Max found out about it, I would get fired and left at the nearest port.

Ahead of Max walked the ship owner's very beautiful, very single daughter, Nellie. In response to something Frank said, she threw her head back, letting out a laugh I knew from experience was throaty and very sexy. Where Nellie went, heads turned. I couldn't begin to compete with her, even if doing so wouldn't cost me my job. As I watched, she reached out and touched Frank on the shoulder. He slung one arm around her casually in an intimate gesture. My heart sank.

Time for this particular fantasy to sail off into the horizon.

W ant to read on? Visit www.lauraheffernan.com and sign up for my newsletter to get it delivered within minutes.

ALL'S FAIR IN LOVE AND BOARD GAMES

Read on for a preview of

She's Got Game

now available from your favorite retailer.

Part I: Boston

Gallivanting Gwen
   June 9

wan-der-lust: /n/ a strong, innate desire to rove around or travel

If home is where the heart is, my home is an airplane. Crisp, clean sheets in an unfamiliar room. Finding the hidden gems in a new city. I've had this blog for almost a year now, and the most common question I get is: why do you do this? Where's your home base?

Well, readers: I do this because I love it. Nothing makes me as happy as strapping into an airplane seat, leaning back, and dreaming about where I'll land. I can recite the safety demonstration along with the flight attendant. I've touched down in thirty-eight states (including Alaska and Hawaii), and I can't wait to see the rest. My best friend Holly doesn't understand how I can stand airplanes, because the coffee's so gross. Here's the secret: coffee's always gross. Diet Coke tastes the same up in the air as on the ground, even if it pours slower on a plane. (See? I'm full of fun facts, thanks to my travels.)

As a kid, we never went anywhere. Dad worked all the time, and it was just the two of us. We didn't have a lot of extra money. He never wanted to take time off. If I had to name a home base, it would be his place. A couple of boxes with my name on them are currently living in his basement. But I have no interest in owning a home, and there's no lease with my name on it.

Someone pass the avocado toast, please. This millennial has no problems with her life. The American dream, it's a-changin'.

This week, I'm back in my old stomping grounds. Ever since the year it rained 28 out of 30 days, I've avoided Boston in June. However, I'm excited to be participating in the annual American Explorers of Islay Board Game Competition. Love this game.

The conference center buzzed with anticipation. Palpable excitement filled the air. Some of the other participants fidgeted. I stood alone, an island of calm in the sea of activity. Nerves were for the less prepared. I'd done my homework, I'd played endless games, and I planned to make it to the final table in Las Vegas, where I'd win the $10,000 grand prize.

In about six months, anyway. One thing at a time.

My first game started in about twenty minutes, leaving me plenty of time to sip my Diet Coke and survey the competition. If someone said "I'm going to the local American Explorers of Islay Competition," most people would picture a room full of pasty twenty-ish guys with glasses and high water pants, living in their parents' basements. We had those types, sure, and my collection of geeky t-shirts fit in perfectly with that crowd. But the room also contained people of all shapes, sizes, genders, and colors, ranging from eighteen to about eighty. We hailed from all over the region, possessed a variety of interests.

And one of us was a very good-looking guy with curly brown hair, surveying me over his coffee cup with gorgeous chocolate brown eyes. He wasn't pasty at all, with a deep tan and lean muscles making his jeans and black t-shirt look a lot more exciting than they sounded. When I met his gaze, he smiled, flashing beautiful teeth, the kind typically found on the wealthy and children of dentists.

Although I'd never seen him before, he chatted with a guy who showed up at these things every now and then. Tall, with thin black braids trailing down his back, the most beautiful light brown eyes I'd ever seen, and dimples. The two of them upped the hotness average in this room by about thirty percent, but both were unfortunately off-limits to me. I didn't date gamers. Don't poop where you eat and all that.

"Not bad." My former roommate, co-competitor, and close friend Holly appeared beside me. "Looking for a little after-competition action?"

I rolled my eyes at her. "Whatever. I won't have the energy for hooking up after I kick butt."

Participants in the American Explorers of Islay Competition competed in a popular resource-sharing board game. The original game accommodated three or four players, and the expansion allowed for more, but the tournament assigned everyone to tables of four. This morning, everyone would play three games and receive a score based on their final rank in each. Table placement was determined in advance by a random draw.

Holly and I weren't playing each other in the first round, but it wasn't a big deal. At some point, we'd inevitably face off. And if we didn't, well, the trash talk would still kick into high gear. The way the tournament was set up, we could both move onto the next round. After three years of grad school and playing together, we'd still be friends after the final scores were announced. It didn't matter whether one of us got knocked out on Sunday or the two of us made it to the final table.

"*Almost* everyone here. I personally plan to wipe the floor with you." Holly corrected me with a wink and a smile. Trash talk and "game hate" ruled at these events. No one meant anything they said. Usually. "Oh, hey, I forgot to mention–last year's winner is here. I talked to him when he transferred his registration from Florida."

With her background and tech know-how, Holly helped set up the registration database for the competition. After years of acting as tech support and back-up registrar, she knew practically everyone's name. We weren't a large community, at least not locally.

Playfully, I swatted at her arm. "What? I can't believe you didn't tell me!"

Last year's winner was a legend. He'd won four years in a row, more than anyone except John, the current competition host. Rumor had it he was calm, collected, and dominated the table during games. Many a gamer imagined testing our skills against C. McKay. The thought of getting to play him here made my mouth water.

Unfortunately, he lived in Florida, so our paths had never crossed. I'd never been able to afford go to the finals. Usually, I volunteered at the local and regional competitions, then dreamed about the rest. But not this year.

"Sorry. Things have been busy with the wedding planning and everything. But there he is."

She pointed at the list of first round match-ups on the wall behind me. Directly below H. McDonald, also known as Holly, the sheet said, C. McKay. A name I'd never seen on the lists in this state, but sent a little thrill through me. Was he as good as everyone said? I couldn't wait to find out.

"Excellent! I can't wait to scope out the competition, find his weak spots, and destroy him."

"You were checking him out a second ago," a voice said behind me.

John, the only person who won more tournaments than C. McKay, stood behind us. He was medium-height, medium-build, probably around my dad's age, with close-cropped, curly dark hair and a salt-and-pepper goatee. Only his whistle and clipboard made him stand out from the rest of the crowd. And the twenty years he'd been around, playing with everyone, making friends. He and his wife Carla co-owned the local game store with his parents, so I'd known him since I was a baby. "That's him over there. Cody."

Following John's finger, my eyes once again landed on the hottie. So that was C. McKay. My number one competition. My ridiculously buff number one competition. My stomach dropped. Why did he have to be an excellent player *and* totally hot? He reminded me of my very first crush as a child, Jonathan Crombie from *Anne of Green Gables* (who reminded me of my second crush, Megan Follows). Those crushes may have played into my utter fascination with the entire series.

He winked at me. For some reason, winking always weirded me out. Maybe because it was mostly old men who did it, looking at twenty-something women. I'd never seen anyone my age do it. As I rolled my eyes, he flashed a grin. My stomach flip-flopped.

Mentally, I revised my assessment: a good player, hot, and a shameless flirt. He probably thought that made him a triple threat. Whatever. I'd been one of only about a dozen females at these events for years: There wasn't a single pick-up line my friends and I hadn't heard. This guy didn't have as much game as he thought.

"Did he wink at you?" Holly rolled her eyes. "Like he's gonna win because he's cute?"

"I think he did."

"If only he frosted the tips of his hair or wore a popped collar, he could be a total walking cliché."

"Or both," I agreed.

A high, clear tone filled the room: the bell, alerting us that we only had ten minutes to get to our tables and settle in before the first game started. The guy started toward us, eyes still fixated on me, and I groaned.

"Ugh. I'm not up for introducing myself."

"I'd love to say hello," Holly said, "but I need coffee before we start."

"Yeah, I've gotta go, too," John said. "Talk to you later."

"You don't want to say hello yourself?" My question went to both of them, but John had turned away, tilting his head the way he did when someone spoke into the earpiece he wore during these events.

True friends wouldn't abandon me with this guy. If he opened with "Hey, is your name Sonic? Because you've been running through my dreams," I'd never forgive them. And, knowing Holly, she'd be sorry to miss such a horrible line. She'd been attached to her fiancé for so long, most everyone around here knew not to bother trying their luck. Every once in a while, though, a newbie got sucked in by her perfectly polished sorority girl look and decided to make a move. Usually with amusing results.

Holly grinned as she stepped away. "Not with the way he's looking at you. See you later."

Before I could argue I wasn't here to flirt, she vanished back into the crowd, and C. McKay arrived in front of me. He looked even better up close, if possible. A wave of disappointment hit me. Part of me hoped he was like a Monet—beautiful from afar, but a total mess up close.

"Carrots?" he said.

As pick-up lines went, this one stumped me. It beat the

Sonic line some creeper tried on me a few months ago, but largely because it made no sense. With no idea what he was talking about, I said the first thing that came into my head. "Squash? Rutabaga?"

He chuckled and pointed at my chest. Oh, right. My t-shirt: *Don't Keep Calm, He Just Called You Carrots.*

My face grew warm. "Sorry, I forgot. It's an *Anne of Green Gables* reference."

"I got the reference. I was trying to be funny. Sorry." He held out one hand. "Cody McKay."

In all the times I'd worn this shirt, no guy my age had ever caught what it meant. Of course, I'd never met a guy who looked like Gilbert Blythe. Under other circumstances, I'd have been impressed. But now I was mostly intrigued to meet the guy I'd heard so much about. Not that he could know. "Gwen Williams. I'll be kicking your ass here shortly."

"Gwen? That's a pretty name." He smiled. "Think I prefer Carrots, though."

My stomach fluttered traitorously at the way he looked at me. My hand tingled where our fingers still touched, but I quashed those emotions. If this guy thought he could charm me to throw me off-guard, he had another think coming. Just because he was better-looking than the average gamer didn't mean I'd fall at his feet once he flashed those gorgeous brown eyes. I came here to win games, not to hook up.

Hoping he couldn't see how flustered he made me, I said, "Then maybe you should hit up the snack room. They've got plenty of carrots for you."

"Sorry. I didn't mean to offend you. I'm usually much better at this."

"Well, if you're not great at playing games, you're in the wrong place." I flashed a broad smile at him to take the bite out of my words. "Excuse me, I've got a tournament to win."

"Actually, *I've* got a tournament to win," he said, smoothly maneuvering around me. Still walking, he turned to look back at me. "After all, I'm the four-time American Explorers of Islay Competition champion."

"That's because you've never played against me." The parting shot had the desired effect in that it made him pause for a second. He shook his head, grinning, which left me dying to wipe the smug look off his face.

So that was the guy I needed to beat. He apparently thought charming the other players gave him an advantage. Little did he know, I'd had plenty of experience with silver-tongued gamers who relied on their good looks to get girls. They didn't impress me. Our interaction only made me more determined to hand Cody his ass in a game.

With a small smile, I tugged at my t-shirt, bringing the v-neck a bit lower. My boobs couldn't compete with Holly's, but I could give him something to look at. Then I shook my long hair out of its braid and pressed my lips together to redden them. Two could play Cody's game. But only one of us would win, and it was going to be me.

More by Laura Heffernan

The Reality Star Series

America's Next Reality Star: Jen went on a reality show to compete for the $250,000 grand prize. But when she finds herself battling another woman for co-competitor Justin's love, she finds herself wondering what the true prize is.

Sweet Reality: After a killer competitor threatens her new business, Jen sets sail on a new reality show adventure to save the day. But Ariana's back, and she's determined to end Jen and Justin's relationship once and for all.

Reality Wedding: After retiring from reality TV, Jen receives an offer she can't refuse. The Network wants Jen and Justin to film their wedding to fill an empty time slot—and if they refuse, the Network will get Justin fired.

The Gamer Girls Series

She's Got Game: Gwen's dedicated to becoming the American Board Games Champion, and she never ever mixes gaming with pleasure. But when she meets Cody, trying to resist his charm becomes a losing proposition.

Against the Rules: For years, Holly has harbored a secret crush on her best friend's dad. Nathan is young, he's hot. What's a little harmless flirtation while playing games? But when she discovers that Nathan returns her feelings, Holly may have to choose between two of the most important people in her life.

Make Your Move: Shannon's more interested in designing games and rising to the top at work than dating. She's surprised to find herself falling for her roommate, Tyler. Worse, he's dating her boss's daughter. If she makes her move, Tyler's girlfriend could get Shannon fired.

~

Push and Pole Series

Poll Dancer: A delightfully modern twist on *My Fair Lady*: When a promotional video for her pole-dancing classes goes viral, Mel comes under fire from a local politician running for senate. Desperate to save her studio, Mel decides her only option is to launch her own campaign — and win!

The Accidental Senator: After accidentally finding herself elected state senator, Lana Chen is determined to prove her worth. But when a mistake aids the passage of a bill that's going to put her best friend out of business, Lana has to find a way to set things right before it's too late.

~

Retail to Riches Series

A Royal Farce: After years of secretly crushing on her friend Pierre, Lila is thrilled when he proposes they start a fake relationship. For weeks, she finds herself hoping their farce could turn into the real thing—but Pierre's hiding a secret of royal magnitude.

A Royal Pain: **Coming Soon**

~

Standalone Books

Finding Tranquility: Jess Cooper lost her husband on 9/11. Just not the way she thought. On September 11, 2001, Brett enters Logan Airport bearing a ticket for a flight that crashes into the World Trade Center. Jess knows her husband is gone. She doesn't know he never boarded that plane. Years later, Jess is shocked to meet Christa and recognize her spouse. She's more shocked to realize their love may have survived.

Anna's Guide to Getting Even: Anna's perfect life has turned into a string of disasters: After a hurricane destroys her house, her ex publicizes private photos of her — which costs Anna her job and her current boyfriend. And after hitting rock bottom, she decides that revenge is the only way forward…

Friction: Britt's always avoided relationships. Then, weeks before she's set to move away, she meets Colin. To her surprise, she finds herself wanting more.

Time of My Life: She's a poor dance teacher. He's her rich student. If they can only overcome their differences, this could be love. A gender-flipped update of *Dirty Dancing*.

About the Author

Laura Heffernan writes fun, witty romantic comedies and more serious women's fiction. After a few years of practicing law, she realized she much preferred arguing with her characters rather than other people. It's easier to win that way.

When not watching total strangers get married, drag racing queens, or cooking competitions, Laura enjoys board games, travel, board games, baking, and board games. She lives in the northeast with her husband, the world's most active toddler, and two furry little beasts. Laura loves connecting with readers. Find her on Facebook or on Twitter, where she spends far too much time tweeting about reality TV and Canadian chocolate. Sign up for news and updates at http://www.lauraheffernan.com/.

Welcome to Shady Grove...

Aly doesn't believe in psychics. Too bad she just had a vision.

Future scientists don't have visions. Aly's got enough on her plate, with finishing her degree and taking care of her nephew and starting her new job at the antique store while drooling over the owner's gorgeous son. No visions.

Alas, the universe doesn't care what Aly believes. When she turns 21, she starts to feel psychic impressions left on objects. A disorienting power for someone surrounded by antiques. Then cranky customer Earl is killed, and Aly's new boss Olive is the prime suspect. Who hated Earl enough to kill? Police would rather make a quick arrest than investigate, so it's up to Aly to clear Olive's name.

Shady Grove is reeling from the first murder in decades. If Aly can get her hands on the murder weapon, she should be able to solve the crime. Can she learn to control her visions before the killer sets their sights on her?

Mystic Pieces
The Scry's the Limit
Sight Seering
Seer Today, Gone Tomorrow